"THEY ARE ALL DEAD?"

Regan drifted the helicopter in a low, slow circle. He searched for fire or explosion damage but there was nothing to dispute the original reports. It was just a silent oil rig, the machinery had stalled and nothing moved. The derrick was an elaborate, skeleton-like tombstone sticking out of a perfectly blue sea. Beside one of the thirty or more sprawled bodies a couple of large, scavenging gulls also lay dead.

Regan glanced at Freeman through the toughened perspex face mask of his air-sealed suit. He couldn't help feeling that indirectly the tall army major and his kind were somehow responsible for all this.

"You wanted to come." Freeman was suddenly defensive.

Regan nodded and then looked back to the rig. He felt angry but he knew that it was mostly a psychological reaction to swamp the fear that his mind didn't want to admit was there. His gloved hands were tensed on the control column and it took an effort of will to move the helicopter down toward the landing pad. There were corpses on the pad itself, naked men who had probably been sunning themselves. Regan tried to set the helicopter down decently so as not to crush any of the bodies.

When they came to rest he switched off the engine. The rotor blades spun slowly to a stop, the noise decreasing and then cutting out altogether.

There was silence, the gut-crawling, throat-dried silence of a waiting grave.

Freeman opened the door . . .

COBRA STRIKE

Robert Charles

PINNACLE BOOKS   LOS ANGELES

COBRA STRIKE

Copyright © 1979 by Robert Charles

A Pinnacle Books edition, published by special arrangement with Robert Hale, Ltd.

Originally published in England by Robert Hale, Ltd. under the title *Venom of the Cobra*.

First printing, February 1980

ISBN: 0-523-40089-6

Cover illustration by Paul Stinson

Printed in the United States of America

PINNACLE BOOKS, INC.
2029 Century Park East
Los Angeles, California 90067

ONE

The oil rig stood alone in its own brilliant blue world. The azure seas of the Gulf of Mexico were calm, an eye-aching dazzle that stretched unbroken to the equally vivid blue of the horizon. The giant drilling platform standing clear of the waves on six massive supports was a black and noisy violation of the hot blue stillness of sea and sky. The noon sun blazed directly overhead of the tall steel derrick, a white core in the vast infinity of blue.

Beneath the block and tackle lines of the hoisting gear drilling was in progress. The rotary table turned slowly as it gripped the kelly and drove the long column of steel piping deeper into the sea bed below. The drilling crew wore hard hats and sunglasses but no shirts and sweat dripped from their grease- and oil-dirtied chests as they worked. It was too hot for talk and the job was routine with no need for commands or curses. Except for the rumble and clatter of the essential machinery the men toiled in sun-baked silence.

Half way up the derrick two electricians hung on safety belts as they checked the cables to a pair of arc lamps that had malfunctioned the night before. Drilling was a round the clock job and the lights would be needed again as soon as the sun went down.

On the helicopter landing pad a few men from the off-duty shift sprawled in naked sun worship, but most of the men who had a choice preferred to stay out of the heat.

A faint humming sounded above the noise of drilling. One of the bronzed sun worshippers heard it first and opened his eyes. The drone increased and he heaved himself up on to one elbow to take a look.

The rig was no longer alone. Another intruder had appeared on the horizon to penetrate their blue isolation. A small airplane took shape out of the heat haze and more men sat up to take notice. High on the derrick the two electricians leaned back and shielded their eyes with their hands.

The plane approached steadily, a red and silver Piper Cherokee that was heading directly for the rig. No one recognized the plane but speculation was casual and unconcerned. Any passing pilot was liable to fly close and give them a wave.

A few more men wandered out of the accommodation huts, attracted by any break in the monotony. A cook ventured out of his galley and the radio operator appeared on the deck outside his shack. The drilling crew only paused when they saw that the plane was going to pass directly overhead. It was flying low and they saw that it was fitted with crop-spraying tanks.

As the red and silver airplane passed slowly over the rig clouds of vapor suddenly poured out from beneath the wings. "What the hell!"

"Did you see that?"

"What's that dumb knucklehead think he's doing!"

A dozen upturned faces spoke at once, some alarmed and some uncertain of what they had seen. The vapor cloud was colorless and as the plane swept on no one was really sure of what had happened.

Suspended on the derrick one of the electricians glanced at his teammate.

"Jake," he said dubiously. "I think we'd better get down."

Jake nodded. His own instinct was registering alarm

and he began to unbuckle his safety belt. Half way through he began to cough and suddenly his nose was running, his chest felt tight and his vision began to blur.

"Hey, Mac—" Jake couldn't get the rest of his words out because by then his throat was on fire. He couldn't breathe and sweat poured out of every gland. He was wild-eyed and helpless and nausea was surging up his gullet.

Mac couldn't help him because already he was experiencing the same agonizing convulsions.

The rest of the crew began to panic when the first electrician lost his grip and fell. His flailing body crashed on to the working deck and he was mercifully killed. Dangling from the steel lattice work of the derrick by his safety belt Mac was still writhing and screaming hoarsely.

The radio operator realized that something was hideously wrong. He didn't know what but he knew that he had to make an urgent distress call. He dived for the door of his radio shack but he began to choke before he could reach his transmitter. He couldn't see the array of dials and he staggered and fell over his chair. His muscles cramped and he couldn't get up. He had a sudden blinding headache and he couldn't think. The intended words of his vital *mayday* signal became confused and then swamped by the searing pain waves that engulfed his brain. He poured sweat and spewed vomit, and although he didn't know it he was defecating and urinating at the same time. His convulsions lasted for thirty seconds before he died.

All over the rig men were screaming, staggering and falling. Those who dived for shelter and tried to lock doors and windows behind them found no escape. Those who tried to scramble lower down the rig prolonged their lives by only a few seconds.

In less than a minute the last twisted body had ceased its violent contortions and the rig was covered by a grotesque confetti of scattered corpses.

3

* * *

The Piper Cherokee flew a wide circle over the sea and then turned back, climbing to gain a safe altitude as it passed over the rig for the second time. The three men in the small cabin looked down on their work with satisfaction and no compassion.

Rashid, the pilot, was a fierce young man with a hot temper, but with a steady hand at the controls. Now he was smiling, his white teeth flashing in his brown face.

Beside him was Sharaf, the group commander, a cool-headed, eagle-eyed man who had learned that hate and fury were not enough. At twenty-five he was the oldest of the three.

Rashid and Sharaf had both acquired their military and flight training in Soviet Russia, in the company of a batch of young hawks from the Syrian Air Force. Jemal, the third man of the group had been included because he had learned to speak fluent American in Beirut.

They were Palestine commandos, and the continuing misery of their unwanted and outcast nation had drained them of all human feeling towards the blind and uncaring world beyond the confines of the refugee camps. They had no hope for the future, but repeated terrorism was the mind-boosting drug that helped to keep themselves and their people alive for today. Like addicts to heroin the addicts to terror needed stronger and stronger doses of their drug to survive in their own living hell, and so the terror war went on.

"Cobral will be pleased," Rashid remarked as they circled the rig.

Sharaf nodded, but he was already thinking forward to the next rig that stood twenty miles south, hidden by the hazed curve of the horizon.

"Fly on," he ordered. "We have not finished yet."

Two thousand and seven hundred miles away another rig stood remote and alone. Here the sweltering green

4

wilderness of the Upper Amazon was cut by the turgid brown wriggle of a wide river, a tributary of the Maranon. The rig stood on a beachhead of yellow sand that had been widened by an army of men with machetes. Designed in two-ton sections that had been airlifted in to the location by helicopters the rig had been welded together on the spot.

There were uncounted millions of barrels of oil beneath the tangled swamps and forest of the Amazon, and now that the Arab oil sheikhs had jacked up the price of world oil there was renewed interest and the scope for profit in the more inaccessible of the earth's oil basins. This American-owned rig, cut off by green barriers of snake-infested jungle, was part of the new spearhead for the great multinational Amazon oil rush.

The helicopter appeared unexpectedly out of nowhere. Its shadow fell over the rig as it hovered with the big blades whirling. Men stared upwards and waited for it to land. It wasn't a company helicopter, but there were any number of freelance pilots cashing in on the almost unlimited demands for choppers and so the rig crew assumed that they had a legitimate visitor, or that base had managed to arrange an additional supply drop.

Then the colorless, odorless, but deadly gas vapor was pumped out over the doomed rig.

The helicopter whirled on. The men below died in the same horrible agony as their predecessors in the Gulf of Mexico. Like demented ants in a nest that had been savagely kicked open they tried to run in all directions as the first symptoms took effect. The area around the rig was full of men screaming, staggering, falling. Their bodies heaved and jerked and twitched in uncontrollable muscle spasms. They beat at the earth with fists or clawed at it with fingers. They died retching with helpless bowel and bladder movements that left them with no human dignity.

* * *

5

The helicopter came back.

The two men and the woman who looked down on the dead rig were all Japanese, insane fanatics of Japan's Red Army. Their organization had pushed itself into prominence in the merciless arena of world terrorism with the bloodiest atrocities of all, possibly because theirs was the least definable cause.

For Kanin Hisato and Jiro Masaka, the pilot and copilot of the helicopter, terrorism was an end in itself. In terrorism they found a perverted glory, and a distorted dream of honor in the ancient warrior traditions of the *samurai*. For them it was a better alternative to becoming docile, robot servants of one of the giant business firms that dominated Japan, apeing the customs and manners of the capitalist Americans they hated, and forsaking any identity or culture of their own.

Their leader was Yaeko Ishida, a woman whose heart was as bitter as her face was beautiful. She had long black hair and a slim, feminine body that no man would ever know. Once Yaeko Ishida had been in love and on the point of marriage, but then the parents of her intended husband had learned the terrible truth that she had tried to keep secret, and they had forbidden the wedding. The man whom Yaeko had loved had been sent north to Nikko and an obscure branch of his father's firm and she had not seen him again.

The terrible truth was that years before Yaeko Ishida had even been born her parents had lived on Kyushu Island, not far from the city of Nagasaki. They had been far enough away to survive the atomic blast that had ended World War Two by wiping Nagasaki from the face of the earth, but also they had been close enough to be horribly scarred and disfigured by the blistering waves of heat and radiation from the fireball. Their mutilation was plain to see, but what deformities might exist inside the child they later conceived, or might later appear in the child of that child, were too fearful to imagine.

6

The parents of the man Yaeko Ishida should have married were terrified of the possibility that their grandchildren might prove abnormal, and when their son was told he too was unable to face the thought that he might become the father of a mutant with two heads or shrivelled limbs.

After that cruel and humiliating experience Yaeko Ishida had determined that she would never love again. And with no love in her heart there was only room for hate. She hated the parents who had conceived her. She hated the bright new Japan which had so quickly forgotten the horrors of Nagasaki and Hiroshima in its frantic efforts to imitate the despised conquerors. And most of all, violent, malignant and all consuming, was the hatred she bore for the imperialist monsters who had sent their warplanes to drop the atomic bombs on the old Japan.

Now her only thought as she looked down upon the dead bodies of the American oilmen was that they had not suffered enough.

The third attack took place on the other side of the globe. Here in the wild grey wastes of the North Sea another major oil rush was in furious progress. Millions of pounds had been invested in the gale-lashed seas where men battled continuously against atrocious conditions. The Arctic might be colder and the occasional Gulf hurricane more violent, but for sheer bloody-minded, wave-pounding, foul-weather persistence the North Sea was in a class of its own.

Arturo Vincenzi looked down on the sullen grey waves that were heaving in a long swell below and he was almost afraid. He was a hot-blooded young man who would have willingly died in the hills and jungles of his native Venezuela, but the thought of drowning in these icy, alien waters was not so pleasant. A squall of rain blurred his vision and the helicopter was pushed

7

sideways by a gust of wind and he had to concentrate on handling the controls.

Luis Cobral felt the helicopter lurch and glanced at his pilot's face. He thought Arturo looked pale but then decided it was probably the excitement that was the grand climax after all the long months of planning and preparation. Cobral could feel excitement coursing like a stimulant through his own veins and despite the wet, grey world around them he had never felt more vibrant and alive. He smiled at Vincenzi, the smooth, handsome smile that had served him well with a long succession of impressionable young women. His perfect teeth flashed white in his dark-skinned face and there was a gleam in his dark olive eyes. Vincenzi became aware of the smile and grinned faintly in return.

"Over there!"

Orlando Savas leaned forward between Vincenzi and Cobral and pointed ahead and slightly to their left. There the squat, derrick-crowned bulk of an oil production platform was taking shape through the grey murk of rain, ragged clouds and running seas.

"Target One," Cobral said with satisfaction.

Vincenzi banked the helicopter in a half turn and they closed rapidly. The rig reared up before them, a vast, rainswept monument to man's ocean enterprise, the tower of the derrick stabbing the low cloud and the crane jibs brooding like black sentinel beaks over the working decks. Faces twisted up to watch but Cobral knew that the men below were unsuspecting. The great North Sea oil bonanza was still making headline impact with the British news media, and so the oil rigs had grown accustomed to the sight of helicopters loaded with TV cameramen and reporters circling over their heads.

A few men waved and Cobral smiled briefly and waved back casually with his left hand. With his right hand he operated the lever that opened the spray nozzles on the gas tanks.

8

The strong winds gave Vincenzi some difficulty in bringing the helicopter round for the second time. However, Cobral's timing had been perfect and the steady rain had quickly carried the deadly vapor down to blanket the rig. When they returned there was no one left alive.

"Target Two," Cobral said calmly and Vincenzi set the new course.

Five minutes later they whirled low over the next rig and again the deadly gas was pumped out over the upturned, raw and rain-streaming faces of a crew of doomed men. Cobral was smiling broadly as he looked back through the port side window and then he heard Savas let out a hiss of alarm.

"Luis," Savas exclaimed sharply. "There is a ship down there."

Cobral twisted round in his seat, leaning back so that he could see behind Vincenzi's shoulders and through the starboard window where Savas was pointing. Below them a small trawler was pitching heavily through the long seas. A curtain of rain almost masked the vessel from view, but for a few seconds Cobral saw a white face staring up from the wheelhouse and he knew that the man at the wheel must also have heard and seen their helicopter.

Cobral cursed. He had not expected to find a ship on the blind side of the rig but now he had to assume the worst. The trawler was probably a patrol vessel that had been hired by the oil company to keep other fishing boats and unwanted visitors a safe distance away. If her captain suspected that something was wrong and then failed to raise the rig by radio contact an alarm would be raised that could prevent the helicopter from making a safe return to its base. Cobral was not prepared to take that risk.

"Arturo," he snapped. "Turn back quickly over the ship."

Vincenzi banked the helicopter in a sharp, low turn

and Cobral twisted again in his seat. However, he had no need to instruct Savas who was already struggling to open the door. Cobral leaned back to help him and when their efforts had succeeded an icy blast of wind and rain ripped inside. Cobral held the door open while Savas thrust the black muzzle of the submachine gun that he had lovingly nursed all the way from Venezuela through the crack.

Two men had emerged on the deck of the trawler and were staring up. One of them held a pair of binoculars but seemed uncertain whether he should focus them on the returning helicopter or the rain-veiled rig. A third face, that of the helmsman, was still visible behind the smeared glass of the wheelhouse.

Vincenzi took the helicopter low, the blades beating down a force of wind that caused the two men on the trawler's deck to duck before they could realize what was about to happen. Then Savas opened fire and the bullets toppled the two men and chewed out a flying nightmare of blood and flesh and splinters along the trawler's deck. The face at the helm disappeared behind an explosion of glass.

The helicopter roared on.

With no hand at the helm the trawler began to swing broadside to the wind. She rolled helplessly and the first of the big seas began to break and cascade over her starboard bow.

Savas was smiling, an eager, soft-mouthed smile of pure pleasure. His slim body was trembling and he breathed the stink of cordite as though it was some rare and exotic perfume.

"We should go back," he said. "Give them another burst to make sure."

"No," Cobral was looking over his shoulder and he could see that the trawler had started to drift at the mercy of the waves. "They were all killed and the sea will finish the ship. Our fuel is low now and we have no more to waste."

Vincenzi nodded agreement, for he was worried that the weather might get worse. They were flying at the extreme limit of their range and now he headed back towards the north coast of Scotland.

Savas was disappointed that he had only been allowed to fire off one magazine from his submachine gun, but Cobral was well satisfied with their day's work. He hoped that the other groups he had trained had proved equally successful.

Luis Cobral, code-named the Cobra, was the mastermind behind the new worldwide operation that had been financed by the nebulous consortium of Terror Incorporated. Oil was the undisputed life blood of every established modern society, and so Terror Incorporated had vowed to attack that life blood at every source.

TWO

Seen from the open window of the luxury apartment building on the New Jersey bank of the Hudson the multi-towered glitter of Manhattan was beginning to blaze at its brightest against the night sky. The monolithic slabs of jewelled and glass-plated concrete were reflected in the dark flow of the river and to the west the constant streams of traffic, muted by the distance, purred softly over the George Washington Bridge.

Lydia Regan stared out over a bourbon on ice in a pensive mood. She was a tall woman with long ash-blond hair that would gleam silver in the right kind of moonlight. It was a warm evening and she felt overdressed in a blue nylon slip. She toyed with the idea of taking it off but Steve usually liked to do that for himself.

She heard the shower stop running, and a few minutes later the bathroom door opened behind her. Lydia didn't look round.

"Sometimes I wonder just how much more Manhattan can take," she said wryly. "You'd think that one more bulb would fuse the whole damned issue, or that one more skyscraper would sink the entire island!"

Firm brown hands rested on her bare shoulders.

"I guess somewhere some power-brained egghead has worked out just how far they can go before that happens," Steve Regan assured her.

Lydia turned then to look at her husband. At forty-

13

five Steve Regan was still as physically fit as any youth of twenty, but now he was a whole lot heavier and harder. His face was square, rough-cast as though it had been shaped to bulldoze rather than charm its way through life, but it was compensated by an even grin and deep blue eyes. His black hair was combed straight back but never quite stayed in place. Now it was tousled after a brief rub with the towel that was knotted loosely around his waist.

"You're not dressed. Does that mean we're not going out?"

"I hadn't planned anything. Had you?"

"Maybe. But maybe I can think of something else." She smiled and curled her finger in the dark hairs on his chest. "Who wants to put clothes on anyway?"

Regan pulled her close and kissed her. Lots of things had changed over the twenty years that they had been together. With the Air Force they had lived in Europe, Korea, Japan and Vietnam. Then Regan had been recruited by the CIA, returning to Tokyo, and then on to Beirut. Now they were back in New York, but between Lydia and himself nothing had ever changed. She was still as hot to jump into bed with him as a young bride. The only difference was that now she didn't close her eyes. They were large grey eyes that smiled into his own as they kissed.

They were still embraced when the radio alerter interrupted them with its shrill *bleep, bleep, bleep!*

Lydia jumped and bourbon splashed out of the glass she was holding and spilled over Regan's shoulder.

"Damn that thing!" she said with feeling as he broke away.

Regan crossed to the bed where he had thrown his pants. The radio was clipped to his belt and he pressed the speech button to kill the bleeping.

"Regan here," he said briefly as he shook the pants away.

"Sorry to disturb you, Colonel." The voice was polite

but unhesitant. "This is Hanson. Something's come up that I think you ought to know about."

"Can't it wait until morning?"

"No, sir. First reports suggest Mike-Tango-Alpha."

Mike-Tango-Alpha—MTA—Major Terrorist Attack. Detective Lieutenant Roy Hanson could not have spelled it out more clearly.

"Here or abroad?" Regan demanded.

"Here and abroad."

"I'll be right over."

Lydia found his shirt and threw it to him.

"If that thing had eyes," she said, "I'd scratch them out!"

Less than thirty minutes later Steve Regan was at New York Central Police Headquarters, hurrying up to the top floor suite of offices that had been cleared to house Counter-Terror, the western security network that had been created to deal specifically with international terrorism. A grizzled police captain watched him pass with a scowl. There were a few old-fashioned cops who didn't approve of this new outfit occupying part of their premises, but it was something they had to learn to live with. Counter-Terror was a parallel to Interpol, plugging the political gap that Interpol left wide open. In addition to being an investigative task force Counter-Terror was also an early warning terrorist information exchange between New York and all European police forces using specially released Interpol radio channels.

Regan reached the main office that was cluttered with desks, chairs, typewriters and old-fashioned filing cabinets. To his left was the communications room where a constant radio watch was maintained to receive incoming reports from London, Paris, Munich and Rome. He could hear voices in there and moved towards them, but then Hanson came out of the main filing room where brand new computer banks stored every available scrap of terrorist information.

15

Detective Lieutenant Roy Hanson was tall and lean with sand-colored hair cut short and horn-rimmed glasses that gave him the image of a fast rising young executive. He moved as though he was forever cutting seconds or corners in order to pack the maximum amount of action into any one day. He headed the team of detectives who handled the office routine, monitoring all incoming and outgoing reports.

Behind Hanson appeared a larger, heavier figure, a six-foot Negro with massive shoulders who walked more lazily but who was capable of outrunning Hanson in a sprint if ever he put his mind to it. FBI Agent Wayne Johnson wore a dark blue suit, pale blue shirt and a blue silk tie. Regan guessed that the radio alerter had hauled him out of a nightspot, somewhere where the atmosphere was soul music and the T-bones were double size.

Counter-Terror was basically a police network, but it needed the full cooperation of all intelligence and law enforcement agencies. So far the main exponents of terrorism had been of Arab or Japanese origin, and so a top CIA man with a working knowledge of both Arabic and Japanese, plus four years of intelligence experience in the Middle East, had been the ideal choice as Counter-Terror Section Head for New York. A senior field office director of the FBI had proved the ideal second in command.

"What's happening?" Regan asked.

"The reports are on your desk," Hanson told him. "The entire crews of two oil rigs in the Gulf of Mexico have been wiped out. A shore station tried to make a routine radio contact with one of the rigs at thirteen hundred hours, our time. They couldn't raise the rig so eventually they sent a helicopter out to check. All they found was dead men, sprawled everywhere. There was no sign of fire, no sign of explosion. The chopper pilot flew a high circle. His buddy used a pair of binoculars and states that there was no blood on any of the dead

16

men, but their faces and bodies were horribly twisted. The pilot decided that he didn't dare put down. They made a radio check on all the rigs in the area and got silence from the next rig down the coast. They checked that one too and it's the same story. So far that's all the details we have."

"You said here *and* abroad!" Regan reminded him.

"Sure, there's a separate report from the Counter-Terror office in London, signed by Superintendent Nicolson. They've had something similar happen to a couple of their offshore rigs in the North Sea. It seems they lost a helicopter pilot too. The guy couldn't raise the rig when he flew over so he put the chopper down to find out what was wrong. The weather was bad out there. He could see bodies through the rain and figured there had been an accidental explosion of some kind that had knocked out the rig radio. His own radio went silent one minute after he'd touched down on the landing deck."

"So the Gulf pilot made the right decision. Where did the Gulf report originate?"

"Galveston Police Headquarters."

"Warn them. Make sure they know what happened to that chopper pilot in the North Sea. Make sure our chopper pilots keep on making the right decisions."

Hanson nodded and headed back to the radio room.

"This could tie in with the earlier reports we had today," Johnson said slowly. "Last night there were three separate terrorist attacks on major land oil installations in Venezuela: a refinery, a bunch of storage tanks and another drilling rig were all blown up, and the fires from the first two are still raging. It's the first really bad outbreak of guerrilla activity that they've had for several years."

"It figures," Regan conceded. "After embassies and airliners, oil has always been a favorite terrorist target."

"I had Hanson get a computer read-out just before you arrived. There's a long list of oil attacks in Europe and the Middle East. Storage tanks in Tripoli were blown up a few years ago. In April '73 a group of eighteen armed men attacked an American refinery at Sidon in Lebanon and temporarily halted pumping operations from Saudi Arabia. There have been attacks on the oil pipelines in Iraq, and there was a combined attempt by Japanese and Arabs to blow up the main oil installations at Singapore. There was that hijacked supertanker that another combined group almost blew up in Rotterdam, and that Red Army–IRA attack on Canvey Island in England. One of our more recent reports from Paris details bomb explosions and major oil fires at two large plants in southeastern France. Counter-Terror in Paris is still hunting for a communist terror group calling itself the Direct Workers Action Committee."

"All scattered in time and place," Regan said. "But the supertanker and the Canvey Island raid were definite operations sponsored by Terror Incorporated, and this has the same smell. Europe and America are dependent upon oil, and our supplies are vulnerable. The Arabs knew that when they jacked up oil prices to force the West against Israel. It makes sense for Terror Incorporated to keep on hitting us through oil."

Hanson came back looking grim.

"Another report, Colonel. It's just been passed on from Langley, Virginia, marked for your personal attention. A CIA agent in Lima, Peru, has just reported that they've got another dead oil rig down there in the Amazon. Again it's a story of mysterious corpses, with no visible structural damage to the rig."

"The Gulf of Mexico, the North Sea and now the Amazon. My money says it's all linked together and we've got to move fast before it happens again."

Regan's voice said jump but Hanson didn't move.

"It's already arranged, sir. I've reserved two seats on the next flight to Houston. You'll be in Galveston before dawn."

* * *

Hanson was not far wrong, for daylight was only just breaking in from the Gulf when a fast state police car rushed Regan and Johnson along the superhighway that connected Houston with Galveston city and island. Both men had grabbed a few hours sleep during the flight and now they were wide awake. The Gulf sunrise was a colorful beginning, splashing great streaks of pink and crimson across the horizon, but it went unappreciated.

Regan used the car radio to contact Galveston Police HQ and learned that all the action was taking place at the oil company shorebase on Galveston Bay. He told the police officer at the wheel to take them straight there and the man nodded laconically.

When they arrived they found a helicopter ready to take off with more than a dozen men gathered around. Some were police officers, some were oil company troubleshooters, and three looked like spacemen in zipped-up silver suits.

The laconic driver stopped the car and Regan and Johnson climbed out. A grey-haired police captain moved to meet them.

"I'm Stratton," the grey-haired man said. "This business was dumped in my hands because I police this area, but you're welcome to it. Crime I know. Homicide, robbery, arson, punk kids and real hoodlums, I can handle them all. This kind of thing you can keep."

"Regan," Regan said as he shook hands. "And Johnson."

"And who the hell are you?"

The heavy, bull-necked man who made the demand looked as though he had spent a lot of sleepless hours just tearing his hair and dragging at the mauled knot of his necktie. He hadn't shaved and his jaw was black.

"This is Mr. Timmerman," Stratton said wearily. "He's the field manager for this depot and responsible for the affected rigs."

"We're police officers," Regan said, as though they were no more than that.

19

"More cops!" Timmerman ranted. "Where the hell does that get us? When is somebody gonna tell me what's happened out there on my rigs? I've got over sixty men out there and all any of you can tell me is that they're all dead."

"We'll tell you more when we know," Regan said calmly, and then moved past him.

Timmerman wanted to say more. He started to follow but then Johnson smiled at him amiably and made a negative move of his head. Timmerman stared uncertainly at the big Negro and then decided that maybe he wouldn't push these two men after all. Johnson strolled after Regan.

Regan had approached the three men in the silver suits. Two of them looked to the third for a lead. The third man was tall with unblinking, uncompromising eyes. A nametape with the name Freeman was sewn on to the left breast of his suit.

"Who are you?" Regan asked.

"An expert," Freeman said carefully.

"An expert at what?"

"Perhaps I shouldn't tell you."

Regan flashed his identification.

"This job is my department," he stated bluntly. "With all due respect to Police Captain Stratton, I am now the top man around here. Everybody tells me everything."

Freeman nodded slowly and drew him to one side.

"Chemical warfare," the tall man said quietly. "The two men with me are research technicians. We flew down from Edgewood, Maryland, last night."

Regan had heard of Edgewood Arsenal in Maryland, a center for research on lethal nerve gases and the preparation of suitable delivery systems.

"You think that what's happened out there is in your line of business?"

"Let's just say that I think I'm best fitted to investi-

20

gate. Last night a supply ship tried to approach one of the affected rigs. They got within a hundred yards before the skipper and his helmsman developed headaches and began to feel sick. The skipper turned back fast. None of his crew died but it's my guess that they got a reduced, partially dispersed dose of whatever hit the rig. That's when my team was called in."

"So what do you plan to do now?"

"We're flying out to the rig. I want some air samples for analysis, and at least one of those bodies for a detailed medical examination."

"Okay," Regan approved. "But I want to examine that rig. Can you find a couple of those protective suits for Agent Johnson and myself?"

Freeman frowned. "I've got to have space for a body and I don't want to leave either of my technicians. Maybe I can take one of you."

"You can take both," Regan said. "I can fly the chopper so we'll dispense with the pilot."

The helicopter pilot was only too glad to stand down. He didn't have a hero-complex but he did have a wife and three kids. He climbed out of the cabin and stripped off the suit he had been given with almost indecent speed. Regan put it on. Another suit was found for Johnson and they were ready to go. Regan took the helicopter up and they whirled out into the sunrise.

Fifteen minutes later they were over the first of the dead oil rigs. Regan drifted the helicopter in a low, slow circle. He searched for fire or explosion damage but there was nothing to dispute the original reports. It was just a silent oil rig, the machinery had stalled and nothing moved. The derrick was an elaborate, skeleton tombstone sticking out of a perfectly blue sea. Beside one of the thirty or more sprawled bodies a couple of large, scavenging gulls also lay dead.

Regan glanced at Freeman through the toughened

perspex face mask of his air-sealed suit. He couldn't help feeling that indirectly the tall army major and his kind were somehow responsible for all this.

"You wanted to come." Freeman was suddenly defensive.

Regan nodded and then looked back to the rig. He felt angry but he knew that it was mostly a psychological reaction to swamp the fear that his mind didn't want to admit was there. His gloved hands were tensed on the control column and it took an effort of will to move the helicopter down towards the landing pad. There were corpses on the pad itself, naked men who had probably been sunning themselves. Regan tried to set the helicopter down decently without crushing any of the bodies.

When they came to rest he switched off the engine. The rotor blades spun slowly to a stop, the noise decreasing and then cutting out altogether.

There was silence, the gut-crawling, throat-dried silence of a waiting grave.

Freeman opened the door.

THREE

Strachan Castle was a lonely, storm-lashed ruin perched on a clifftop on the wild Caithness coast of northern Scotland. On the seaward side the sheer walls of rock dropped straight down for two hundred feet to meet the pounding waves of the North Sea that foamed in grey-white fury for most of the year. The North Sea was rarely calm. On the landward side the castle had once been defended by fifteenth-century walls that had now crumbled into a massive jawbone of gapped and broken teeth. Beyond the collapsed ramparts the ground sloped down sharply, wild slopes that were tangled with rocks and gorse and heather, disappearing into a wilderness of forest. The castle was only partially habitable, but it was occupied.

Hamish Strachan of Strachan, the last Earl of a small but dying clan, looked down from a high window of the south wing. Below him lay the ruins of the great hall. The roof no longer existed and only the walls were standing. At one end of the great hall a large grey canvas tent had been erected and a dozen or more young people of both sexes lounged around it. They were un-washed, dressed in a weird assortment of ragged clothing, draped with blankets or Mexican-type capes, and adorned with a variety of outlandish hats. Most of them were drinking beer or cheap wine, one or two couples were mauling each other in casual sexual embrace, and one youth was playing a guitar.

They were celebrating because the helicopter had returned. The last Earl of Strachan had heard the powerful whirling of the big rotor blades and had painfully propelled his wheelchair over to the window to watch. The helicopter had settled on the wide, flat area of grass between the great hall and the outer walls that had once been the castle courtyard. The unwashed hairies and their tramp girl friends had cheered as it landed and had then helped to move it quickly out of sight into the old stables that still survived along the inside of one of the more solid sections of the decayed jawbone.

Hamish Strachan continued to watch through grimly tightened lips. His gnarled hand itched to grasp a heavy stick, or even a claymore that would scatter this arrogant young filth from his ancient home. He had come to hate them and still he did not understand why Duncan and Fiona had chosen to turn Strachan Castle into a hippie commune. At first he had merely been bitterly disappointed in his son and daughter, believing that they had become as lazy and degenerate as their new friends. Then the helicopter had arrived one black night and he had realized that they did have a purpose.

What that purpose was he could not guess. He had found the following morning that his telephone was disconnected. The lines had probably been torn down by the wind, Duncan had told him. The same day Fiona had stopped bringing his daily newspaper. There was a printing strike, she had said. Duncan had also borrowed his radio and failed to return it. The radio had broken down and was still awaiting repair was the explanation for that. The Earl was no fool and knew they had deliberately cut him off from the outside world.

There was a movement by the stables and the old man moved his eyes to observe. He saw that the three dark-skinned foreigners who had flown the helicopter on its mysterious mission had emerged with Duncan. These three he knew instinctively were the real evil here. Duncan and his crazy friends were mere tools who were being used.

Hamish Strachan gripped the arms of his wheelchair with the fury of helpless frustration. His teeth grated and his jaw ached. Two years ago he had slipped on the steep, grassy slope outside the castle and as he rolled violently downwards a knuckle of rock had smashed him at the base of the spine. Since that day he had been totally paralyzed below the waist and now he was confined and powerless in his chair.

Unaware of the malevolent eyes that glared down on him from the small window high above, Luis Cobral had every reason to feel well satisfied. The heavy rain had followed the helicopter all the way back to the Caithness coast, not clearing until they were within a mile of Strachan Castle. He was certain they had not been spotted, either from the sea or from the air, which meant that the first strike of Operation Cobra had been a total success.

"We can refuel and refill the VX tanks whenever you say the word," Duncan Strachan told him with an equal satisfaction. "The weather report for tomorrow is good, more gales, more rain, and more low visibility. You can wipe out another couple of rigs."

"That sounds perfect," Savas turned on his wide, soft-mouthed smile and looked to Cobral for approval.

"No," Cobral said firmly, knowing that these two had to be restrained. "Our stocks of VX are not unlimited and we must use it to achieve the maximum effect. It is best if we space out our attacks as much as possible."

Strachan frowned and Savas looked petulant. They were two totally different types. Orlando Savas was as slender as a girl, with a girl's mouth and a girl's curling eyelashes. Once he had been pleased to be described as a beautiful boy, but over the years his beauty had turned sour. Beside him Duncan Strachan was a burly

25

young man with thickset shoulders, wild black hair and a full black beard. Beautiful was not a word to describe the young Scot, but virile might have sufficed.

"But why?" They spoke together with one voice.

"We have destroyed the men on two oil rigs," Cobral said patiently. "Try to imagine what will happen now. The word of those attacks will spread until they reach every rig and production platform in the North Sea. It will produce panic and uncertainty. There will be labor disputes. Men will refuse to work the rigs without adequate protection. We may even hope for a total strike that will cripple all oil production in the North Sea. The English trade unions are dominated by communists who will not be able to resist an opportunity such as this. We can watch the so-called 'English disease' do our work for us once we have created the correct conditions for it to take hold."

"If that's what you want then the sure way to do it is to hit another couple of rigs tomorrow," Strachan insisted bluntly.

"There is another reason why we should wait," Arturo Vincenzi said quietly. "After today the English government will step up air and sea patrols. We know that they have a near impossible job with oil and gas rigs scattered over the whole of the North Sea, but there is no need for us to accept the increased risk. Such additional patrols cannot be continued indefinitely, and when they are relaxed, that will be the time to strike again."

Savas sighed his disappointment but accepted the superior judgment of his two friends. He had known Luis Cobral, a brilliant left-wing intellectual, for many years. He had respect for Cobral's high-level clarity of thought and expression, which was coupled to a powerhouse of both mental and physical energy and refined into the planning and organizational abilities of a four-star general. Savas also had respect of a different kind for Vincenzi, an ex-lieutenant of the Venezuelan Navy who

26

had fled into the interior after he and other junior officers had failed in an anti-government rebellion. Vincenzi had a long career of guerrilla warfare behind him, and he had taken part in the skyjacking of a Venezuelan airliner long before the insane Arabs of the PLO had made skyjacking a fashionable pastime. Such things gave him a stature that was second only to Cobral.

Duncan Strachan was still unconvinced, but he couldn't fly a helicopter and so he had to let the matter drop.

"All right, Luis, if that's the way you want it then you and your friends can lie low. But now we've started my men want to carry on hitting the English. We want to do something personal for Scotland. We've postponed our plans for blowing up the oil pipeline from Peterhead to Grangemouth for long enough. It's time to put them into operation!"

Strachan's chief lieutenants had drifted over to listen to the conversation. Hugh Cameron had red hair and a red beard, and wore a kilt of the Cameron tartan. Bruce Munro favored the more conventional hippie gear of dirty jeans and denim jacket. The rat's tails of his tangled hair fell across his shoulders. Both of them nodded agreement with Strachan.

"You promised that your New Scottish Liberation Army would delay all military operations until this present operation is over," Cobral reminded them carefully.

"Maybe." Strachan was truculent. "But we didn't promise to wait for ever. We've been waiting a long time for a free and independent Scotland, and there's some of us who think that we've waited too long. Today is a beginning, and we want to play our part."

Cobral concealed his impatience under a diplomatic mask. The hippie commune and this isolated ruin situated so conveniently on the edge of the North Sea provided excellent cover and an ideal advance base. Without them his job here might not have proved possible, and so he needed the continued cooperation of Duncan Strachan and his absurd New Scottish Liberation Army. Compared to such veterans as Arturo Vincenzi and himself they were mere children playing at revolutionaries. He had a deep contempt for them, but at the same time he knew that he could not afford to offend them.

"By road Peterhead is more than two hundred miles south of here," he pointed out reasonably. "Once you have blown the pipeline you have to return, and there are very few alternative roads that you could use. The police will not be slow to set up roadblocks. At the worst it is possible that some of you may be captured. At the best you will be scattered and obliged to take to the mountains on foot. Either way you put our major operation at risk."

"We won't get caught," Hugh Cameron butted in. "We're not stupid."

"I do not doubt your courage and your abilities," Cobral assured them. "But with every military maneuver there is always an element of risk. Operation Cobra is under way, and all I ask is that we bring it to a satisfactory conclusion before another operation begins."

"I don't know." Strachan rubbed at his bearded jaw and looked at his two lieutenants. "We've been waiting and planning for a long time."

"A revolution is not won in a day," Vincenzi said quietly. "I have spent many years in the jungles of Venezuela."

Strachan pursed his lips, a sure sign of frustration. He knew that Cobral and Vincenzi were talking sense, but at the same time he wanted more for himself than just a support role in their operation. He saw himself as a young lion, and he wanted a lion's share of the glory. He had his own grandiose strategy for making Scotland untenable for the English, and for insuring that the revenue from North Sea oil, when it was allowed to flow, would pour into the coffers of Scotland and not England. Scotland as an independent oil power with himself at the military helm was his dream.

"All right," he conceded at last. "We'll wait a few more weeks. But eventually we're going to blow that pipeline. And when we start we'll attack every terminal, refinery and shorebase in the Highlands. The offshore rigs are yours, but the onshore oil industry we'll take care of for ourselves."

"Agreed." Cobral smiled but not too broadly. He had won but it was not politic to let his satisfaction show too clearly. "But now we have something to celebrate. Let us join our friends."

Strachan hesitated for another moment, but then they all began to move together towards the grey stone archway that led into the ruins of the great hall. Inside the hippies, the self-styled soldiers of the NSLA, were rapidly getting drunk. A thin girl who wore a man's shirt, frayed jeans, beads and a rag of ribbon round her blonde hair, detached herself from the main group near the sagging canvas of the tent and swayed unsteadily towards them. In her hand she gripped a bottle of wine.

"Have a drink," Janis Wallace offered with a pale smile. She looked like someone just recovered from a long illness, or just starting down the long dope road to hell. She pushed the bottle towards Cobral.

Cobral took the bottle, tilted his head and drank briefly. Then he handed the bottle back. If he had smiled at her Janis would have melted, and if he had slipped an arm around her shoulders she would have been his for the night, willing to indulge in any sex game he might fancy. Cobral knew that and so he did neither.

Luis Cobral was proud of his sexual prowess and had already proved himself with Janis and most of the girls here. However, sex was just another weapon in his armory, which had to be deployed wherever it could achieve the best results. Tonight another woman was waiting, and it was to his advantage to keep her satisfied.

"Where is Fiona?" he asked Strachan.

The black-bearded Scot didn't answer directly. He had grabbed up the wine bottle that Cobral had returned and was drinking deeply. He waved one hand in the general direction of the castle and made a bawdy wink with one eye.

Cobral left them and Janis Wallace watched him go with jealous fury in her green eyes.

The emotions of Orlando Savas were similar but better hidden. His homosexual attraction for Cobral was intense but frustrated by Cobral's obvious preference for sex with women. He believed that Cobral was unaware of his secret thoughts and so he pretended a defiant manhood that was expressed in his passion for guns and violence. He rarely moved without his precious submachine gun which was his substitute masculinity.

Cobral knew these things and exploited them to the full.

Fiona Strachan was alone in her room. She was twenty-five years old with shining black shoulder-length hair, sharp blue eyes and a superior IQ. At the moment she was also naked. She knew that she possessed a finely shaped, long-legged and unblemished body, and in her view clothes in privacy were only for the ugly and the dirty-minded. When Cobral arrived she handed him a Bacardi with ice and lime. Her own taste was for five star brandy.

"Flesh is beautiful," Cobral said, toasting her with her own favorite expression.

"Especially mine." Fiona smiled at him and then asked, "I saw you talking with Duncan and the others. My bull-headed brother did not look pleased. Was something wrong?"

"He can't wait to liberate Scotland. I had to counsel patience."

30

"Perhaps I should have been down there, but I wanted you to come up here to me."

"I guessed as much. That is why I came."

Fiona smiled. "Don't worry about Duncan, Luis. He can control those weirdos down there because he is physically stronger than they are. But I can control Duncan because I am stronger-willed than he is. Duncan will argue, but your operation is priority and in the end he will do as I say."

"That is a comfort," Cobral said politely.

Fiona drained her glass and lay back on the bed to watch him, her red lips smiling and her eyes wanton. All women had the same basic equipment, but with some it was more exciting than with others and she knew that the dark V of rich, silk black curls that narrowed towards her sex excited him.

"When are you going to take off your clothes, Luis?"

"I was waiting for the invitation." Cobral smiled his handsome, lady-killing smile and put his glass aside.

Fiona watched him strip. She knew that he did not love her, for Luis Cobral was incapable of any true depth of affection for any one woman. That was why he needed continued conquests to sustain his ego. To Fiona that was unimportant because her own sexual athletics were an expression of art more than emotion, and Cobral was both an athlete and an artist.

More important he possessed a brain that was superior to her own and a guerrilla philosophy that was vast strides ahead of the scattered fragments of her own wild revolutionary thinking. Talking with him was almost as mind-shattering as their sex play, and she knew from their long conversations that he had been one of the masterminds behind the great wave of riots, sabotage, skyjackings and piracy that had ripped through Venezuela in the early nineteen-sixties. The triumph of Cuba had almost been repeated, but then the figurehead of the revolution had been assassinated to leave the guerrillas in disarray. Guerrilla activity had declined but Cobral had remained true to his theories of revolution by terror.

The Terror Incorporated had grown to embrace him, to finance him and provide him with a new, world-wide cause. Fiona Strachan was proud to be part of that cause. She had been instrumental in acquiring the VX nerve gas, and also she had helped when Cobral, Vincenzi and Savas had stolen the helicopter that was essential to their plans from an airfield in southern England. She knew that without her he could not have succeeded.

He reared over her and she spread her legs wide to receive him. On his naked chest there was a large, vivid black tattoo of a striking king cobra. The black eyes mesmerized her from the flared hood and the forked tongue and fangs flashed down towards her as his sex stabbed into her own.

Their encounter had begun.

FOUR

The air conditioning at Galveston Police Headquarters stood no chance against the Gulf heat. It was hot inside and both Regan and Johnson had stripped off their jackets and neckties as they worked in the small office that had been hastily cleared to form their temporary base. Regan had guessed that the dead rigs could only have been gassed from the air. A sea attack just wasn't feasible unless some kind of shell had been fired, and there had been no evidence of a shell or shell damage. Johnson agreed that a low flying, low speed aircraft was the most logical form of delivery and so they had launched a massive enquiry to check out every airfield and every small private plane within a radius of three hundred miles. That was a big chunk of Texas, but they had the full cooperation of every law enforcement agency in the state, including the FBI field director based in Houston.

The telephones were constantly ringing and neither of them heard the brief knock on the door. Freeman came in anyway and sat down on the only spare chair.

"I'll call you back," Regan said and put down his telephone.

Johnson terminated his own conversation in the same moment and they both looked at Freeman. The army major stared back without blinking.

"You sure know how to take your time," Regan said. "What's the verdict?"

"You can't hurry a complete post-mortem examination, especially when we have to protect ourselves from a heavily contaminated body."

"The verdict?" Johnson repeated.

"Much as I had guessed from the symptoms shown by the crew of the supply ship that turned back. The man we retrieved from the rig died from a massive overdose of one of the toxic V agents, the family of organic-phosphorus compounds that were first isolated by British researchers in 1952. The V stands for venomous. A pinhead-sized drop absorbed by the skin is fatal and causes death within minutes, sometimes seconds, depending upon the strength of the subject's heart and central nervous system."

"A nerve gas," Regan said bluntly.

"In plain language, yes."

"The kind of stuff you amuse yourself with at Edgewood Arsenal in Maryland, and at Fort Detrick in Maryland, and Dugway in Utah. You'd better complete that list for me, Major, because I intend to run a thorough security check on all those places."

"Fort Detrick is a center for biological warfare research," Freeman corrected him. "You can cross that one off your list. You can add the Rocky Mountain Arsenal at Denver, Colorado, and the manufacturing plant at Newport, Indiana. The locations are not classified. Dugway is a desert range proving ground for both chemical and biological weapons. We all remember Skull Valley!"

"The wind changed and six thousand sheep shrivelled up and died," Johnson said softly.

Freeman nodded. "Anyway, that's the full list. I can get you a supplementary list of all the US military bases where nerve gas warheads are stockpiled, but that will take a little time."

"Get it," Regan told him.

Freeman gave him a cold look. "You obviously don't approve of chemical warfare, Colonel, but don't make

34

the mistake of assuming that we're all blind fools. The US Army doesn't exactly allow anyone to wander into a high security area and help himself to a cupful of nerve gas."

"We have a security report on our files which states that over the past four years enough small arms and ammunition has been stolen from US bases throughout the world to equip ten battalions of troops," Regan informed him. "That's fact. Another fact is that somehow a major terrorist group has got hold of a supply of nerve gas."

"Even so, my guess is that this particular agent did not originate in the US," Freeman said calmly. "The British process was passed on to our scientists and it has been manufactured here on a large scale. But our boys have improved the original formula, and the bulk of the nerve gases stocked today have slightly different characteristics. I'll put on record that the man I examined just now was killed by a toxic VX agent of the early type that was developed in Great Britain."

"Is that the first step of a cover-up?" Regan demanded harshly.

"No." Freeman was still cold and unblinking and he showed no sign of anger. "I am as concerned about this as you are, and I agree that there must be an immediate security investigation at every research station and at every army and air force base where nerve gas weapons are stored. The point is that I do not expect any results from these investigations, and I am warning you that we should also be looking elsewhere."

There was silence. Regan felt hostile and he knew that it would be easier to work with this human refrigerator if only he would just once show any kind of emotion. Then there was a knock on the door and Police Captain Stratton came in.

"This was just relayed from New York." He held out a two-page, computer-typed report. "It's marked for your immediate attention."

Regan read it through and then passed it to Johnson.

"It's from the Counter-Terror office in London," he said for Freeman's benefit. "They are now certain that their two rigs in the North Sea were sprayed from a helicopter. A service ship patrolling round one of the rigs was attacked by gunfire before the chopper made its escape. One man survived, the engineer who was below deck when the attack was made. He stuck his head out of a hatchway just in time to see the chopper disappearing through the rain."

"That ties in with our hunch that it was an aerial delivery here," Johnson said. "All this is linked and the people behind it wouldn't want to take the risk of perfecting two forms of attack. Nobody in his right mind would handle this stuff more than was absolutely necessary."

Regan nodded. "Check. We'll carry on looking for a light aircraft, or another chopper."

He looked back to Stratton. "Captain, have one of your men get me New York and a direct line to Detective Lieutenant Hanson at Manhattan Central. I want full information flow kept going on this between all Counter-Terror offices, especially New York and London. Also I'm going to request that every Counter-Terror Section Head in Europe promotes an urgent investigation into the possibility of theft from a research center or military base anywhere in his own territory."

If Freeman was satisfied he didn't show it. He got up to leave and then paused in the doorway.

"One more thing, Colonel. I'd advise that you use flamethrowers and incinerate those rigs from a safe distance."

It was Wayne Johnson who answered. "Go tell that to a man named Timmerman," the big Negro said softly.

Freeman stared at him but made no comment. Then he went out and closed the door.

"He's scared," Regan said with a sudden flash of in-

36

sight. "He'll never show it, but he knows exactly what we're dealing with and he is scared to hell and gone!"

A hundred miles away a battered grey station wagon turned off the main highway and headed up a dirt track. Dust clouded up from the wheels and a disturbed rattlesnake slithered away into a crack in the sun-baked ground. The station wagon bumped and jolted as though the lone man at the wheel was drunk or blind and couldn't see the bad places where the track was rutted or broken away.

Frank Kasler wore a check shirt, denim pants, worn boots, and a Stetson to shade his narrowed eyes from the sun. His creased brown face was unnaturally pale and his moustache drooped over tight-set lips. He sat rigid with his arms stretched out stiff to the wheel. He was staring straight ahead but he didn't see the ribbon of dirt road. All that he saw was the stark headlines of the newspaper that lay on the seat beside him.

Frank Kasler was scared, scared and angry, but mostly scared.

The small ranch house appeared ahead against a background of brush covered hills. It had a dilapidated look and hadn't seen a coat of fresh paint for many years. Kasler slowed the station wagon and took another fork of the track, away from the house. He drove across his own small, private airfield towards the hangar.

He stopped the station wagon on the patch of tarmac in front of the wide wooden building and stared at the closed double doors. His mouth was dry and his hands were slippery on the wheel. Now that he was here he didn't want to get out of the car, and he didn't want to read the paper again.

They had warned him not to go near the hangar.

He swallowed hard and pulled in a deep breath. The hell with it, it was his airfield and his hangar and his plane. He reached for the paper, stuffed it into his hip pocket, and then pushed open the car door and got out.

He hesitated for another moment and then walked slowly over to the big double doors. They were locked but he had a spare key. He turned it in the heavy padlock and then pulled open one of the doors. He eased into cool shadow but he was beginning to sweat.

The red and silver Piper Cherokee, his plane which he used for crop-spraying, hiring himself out to the local farmers and ranchers, was standing in the center of the hangar. Instinct told him not to touch it, but he moved slowly round it in a wide circle. Even in the half light he could see that the letters and numbers along the silver fuselage had a wet gleam and were no longer as neat as before. They had been painted out and a false registration number painted in for the one flight that the plane had made without him. Then the false markings had been painted out again and the original returned.

Kasler felt pressure building up inside his head and a tightness around his chest. He realized that he was afraid to breathe and moved back towards the door. Then he hesitated opposite the six slender silver cylinders that lay in a line close beside the wall. They looked like the air bottles that skin divers used, but he knew now that they did not contain air. His throat was dry and his limbs were laden, but he moved one foot and tentatively touched each cylinder in turn with his booted toe. Four of them were still solid, but the other two rolled and chinked emptily together. Kasler recoiled and stepped away.

"Frank!" The sharp, frightened voice jerked him round and he saw Gloria standing in the doorway. His blonde, heavy-breasted wife wore a brief halter top and shorts and her face was white.

"Frank, for God's sake come out of there!"

"It's my goddamned place and it's my goddamned plane," Kasler said defensively, but he moved towards her.

Gloria caught his wrist and pulled him out, swinging her shoulders against the door to close it. She smelled the liquor on his breath.

"Frank, you've been drinking."

"A man's got a right to drink," he said belligerently. "And I've got a right to know what's happening around here. It's my place and it's my plane, and I've got a goddamned right to know what's going on!"

"It's only our place and our plane under certain terms and conditions. We agreed to them. We didn't have any choice. Let's just leave it at that."

He stared at her, realizing how white she was.

"You're frightened," he accused her. "You're more damn frightened than I am—and you haven't even read this paper yet. You know more about this than I do."

"What does it matter? It's none of our business."

"It is my business. It's my plane. Just look at this!" He clawed the folded newspaper from his hip pocket and shook it open under her eyes. "See what it says about these two oil rigs out in the Gulf. Every man on board was wiped out by some kind of poison gas. Over sixty men dead! And it happened yesterday while those three niggers were out flying my plane!"

"Arabs, Mister Kasler, not niggers. Our homeland is Palestine."

Kasler jerked round again as though he had been lashed with a whip. Sharaf had approached silently behind them and now he was watching them carefully through those hooded, eagle eyes. Over his shoulder Kasler saw Rashid and Jemal moving up without haste from the ranch house.

Kasler's throat was raw and dry, but six beers and several large slugs of bourbon had given him courage. He pushed the newspaper at Sharaf.

"What about this? I want to know what the hell is going on."

"Frank, it's none of our business."

Sharaf ignored the paper. "Your wife is right, Mister Kasler. It is none of your business."

"I still want to know."

Rashid and Jemal reached them. Rashid had a machine pistol slung from his right shoulder which he held casually against his right hip. He held back, but Jamal came closer and glanced briefly at the newspaper.

"We had nothing to do with this," Jemal lied gravely.

"Then what were you doing with my plane?"

"*Our* plane, Mister Kasler." Jemal was polite, his English perfect. "If you will remember, *your* plane was the machine you crashed in a drunken stupor more than a year ago. You were lucky to walk away alive. And you were finished, a drunken pilot whom nobody would employ, with no money to buy another plane. You were broke, on the scrap heap!"

Jemal paused to let the memory sink in, then continued, "Our mutual friends provided you with another plane. All that was asked of you was that we should be able to make the occasional private flight for our own private purposes. All you have to do is to turn a blind eye and ask no questions. A very cheap price for a new airplane!"

"When I made that deal I didn't expect anything like this." Kasler was frustrated and angry. "I thought you'd be using the plane for airlifting dope over the Mexican border, perhaps a getaway after a bank raid, or something like that. This business is something different."

"If you wish to believe that we were smuggling heroin from Mexico, then that is what we were doing," Sharaf said calmly.

Kasler stared at them angrily. He could see the veiled warning in Sharaf's eyes, and the naked threat of the machine pistol that dangled at Rashid's hip. Some of the anger went out of him then, pushed away by the fear that was crowding back in. His throat tasted like he had swallowed down a mouthful of desert and he badly needed another drink.

"Let it drop, Frank."

Gloria was pulling at his arm and he looked down into her face. Most of the colour was back, which meant that she had been more scared of what was inside the hangar than she was of the three Arabs. Her tone was half a plea and half an order. She had got him into this and now he realized that all along she had known more about what was happening than he had. Suddenly he hated her almost as much as he hated the three dark-skinned intruders who had so casually occupied his home.

"Come back to the ranch house," Sharaf suggested shrewdly. "I think that perhaps you need another drink of your American whisky."

It was as though the Arab group commander had read his mind. Kasler wanted to scream no. Deep down he knew that the liquor was his weakness and his real enemy. It was the root cause of everything that had gone wrong. He didn't want to see another bottle or taste another drop, but by God his throat was dry. The craving inside him was a cancerous sponge that demanded its fill.

Sharaf and Jemal moved towards the ranch house.

Gloria pulled at Kasler's arm and he fell into step.

Rashid brought up the rear, smiling and with his hand resting cowboy fashion on the butt of his machine pistol.

Sharaf glanced back once. "In future," he said, "I think it will be best if Mrs. Kasler drives into town to collect the groceries."

FIVE

The London office of Counter-Terror was housed in the twenty-story office block of New Scotland Yard. Its windows looked down Victoria Street towards Parliament Square where bedraggled pigeons sheltered from the rain under the eaves of the Houses of Parliament and Westminster Abbey. The London Section Head was Detective Chief Superintendent Mark Nicolson, a tall, fair-haired man with grey eyes and a strong jawline who sat with his back to the depressing view of the weather. On the desk before him were the latest reports from Counter-Terror in New York.

There were two more men present. Sitting in a straight-backed chair on the opposite side of the desk was Detective Inspector Harry Stone, a solid, blunt-faced man with thinning hair who was Nicolson's executive aide. Standing at ease, betraying the military side of his background, was Sir Alexander Gwynne-Vaughan, KBE and DSO, a large grey-haired man with a clipped white moustache and clear blue eyes who was the over-all Counter-Terror Coordinator for Europe.

Nicolson looked up from the reports.

"There's a chemical warfare expert on the other side of the Atlantic who has identified the gas used in the oil rig attacks as the VX type that was first developed in England," he said slowly. "That rings an ominous bell in my memory. Wasn't there an uproar earlier this year

43

when some idiot at the Defense Department let VX off the official secrets list?"

Stone frowned and thought back. "I believe you're right, sir. The *Sunday Times* printed a front-page insight article on the terror risk involved. It didn't come out who made the blunder, or how it came to be made. But VX was taken off the secret list and the specification was filed in the London Patent Office. The *Times* article caused a panic and the Defense Department had to rectify their mistake. VX was reclassified as secret."

"Mine was one of the urgent recommendations to the Home Office that was responsible for the reclassification," Gwynne-Vaughan said. "As I remember VX was first isolated by researchers working on insecticides for ICI. Some dunce at the Defense Department thought that because we have since discovered a whole range of even greater horrors the original formula could be released for further commercial development. The specification document was removed from the Patent Office within twenty-four hours of the *Times* article being printed."

"Twenty-four hours is long enough."

"For someone to realize its potential and do some private research in the Patent Office?" Gwynne-Vaughan stroked his moustache thoughtfully with a forefinger. "You could be right, Mark."

Nicolson looked to Stone. "Check it out, Harry. Send someone around to the Times Building and get a photostat of that insight article so we know exactly what information was made public. Then check with the Patent Office. If we're lucky they may have a visitor's book that will tell us who consulted their files on the Monday immediately after the *Times* leak. Send Ted Marsh if he's available."

"Marsh is still down in Hampshire, getting the details on that stolen helicopter. I'll send Burnett." Stone named the second of their senior detective sergeants and Nicolson nodded approval.

When Stone had left Gwynne-Vaughan decided to take the vacant chair. He had just arrived from the airport after a tiring round of conferences in Oslo, Munich and Paris and had yet to catch up on the latest developments in London.

"What's this about a stolen helicopter?" he asked.

"A Hiller 360, three-seat cabin, fitted up for crop-spraying. It was stolen from a private airfield over a month ago," Nicolson explained. "The Crime Commander at Criminal Investigation put us on to it. The pilot-owner was murdered when the Hiller was stolen and CI were called in. One of their Murder Squad Superintendents is still down there but so far he's been up against a blank wall. Nobody could think of any reason why anyone should want to steal a crop-spraying helicopter—until now."

"Hampshire's a long way south of Scotland."

"True, but the thieves loaded up every spare fuel can they could find. One refuelling stop would have given them the range and there are plenty of lonely fields and moors where they could have settled down at night."

"I take it that all our other enquiries to find the helicopter that attacked the oil rigs have failed?"

"Correct."

"So we make the logical assumption that the helicopter stolen in Hampshire is the one we want, and that it is now hidden away somewhere in Scotland."

"Correct again."

"They'll need more fuel, Mark. Already they've made one long flight from Hampshire to their base in Scotland, and a second long flight out into the North Sea."

"I've stepped up all onshore as well as offshore security," Nicolson assured him. "There are a number of oil industry shore bases and helicopter stations in Scotland where they could get the right kind of fuel, but if they try it there's a good chance that we'll grab them."

"*They,*" Gwynne-Vaughan repeated as though the

45

word tasted sour. "As yet do we have any indication as to who *they* might be?"

"Negative," Nicolson said grimly. "We know from the attacks in the Amazon and the Gulf of Mexico that there's an international link, so we're looking for terrorists from one of the world networks as well as a local group. So far we haven't found them. To the best of our knowledge there are no IRA cells north of Glasgow, and I can virtually swear that no doubtful Japs or Arabs have succeeded in getting into the country."

"The IRA, the PLO, the Red Army, the Baader-Meinhof group," Gwynne-Vaughan listed them wearily. "They are the original hard-core of Terror Incorporated, but now they'll recruit and exchange terrorist teams with any branch of fanatics anywhere in the world. We could be looking for a group of any nationality."

Nicolson nodded. "That's why our main hope lies in finding the local group involved, or the stolen helicopter. Every policeman in Scotland is on the lookout for strangers or foreigners in his area, and for all the likely places where a helicopter could be kept hidden."

"Is that as much as we can do?"

"We're checking the files on all the known ultra-leftist groups operating in England, the political vandals who have been stirring up strikes and riots, staging protests and demonstrations and so forth. They're a mixed bag of Marxists and Maoists, Trotskyites and pure bloody anarchists, but they do tend to fall into two main streams. There are the militant trade unionists who are determined to wreck our economy by fermenting a strike whenever they calculate that it will do the greatest amount of damage to any particular industry, and there are the student revolutionaries who sabotage the educational system and everything else in any way they can."

Gwynne-Vaughan smoothed down his moustache again, it was a contemplative habit. "There are strikes on the oil rigs over this business. In two cases the oil companies have had to pull out the main work force and leave just a skeleton crew."

"True," Nicolson said. "The union militants will obviously take advantage of this situation where they can. But on the whole the unions are not too firmly established in Scotland, and it's my hunch that the people who must be providing a base and cover for the actual terrorist team will probably have their roots in the universities."

"So you're hunting for militant students, or ex-students with a Scottish background?"

Nicolson nodded. "There's one name that springs to mind from a file I studied yesterday, a lad named Hugh Cameron. He led a nasty assault on a visiting professor at the London School of Economics, simply because they didn't like what they termed the capitalist tone of his lecture. He also organized mobile task forces to reinforce the armies of flying pickets that roamed the country enforcing strikes a few years ago. He's dropped out of the picture just lately. He hasn't been seen around his usual haunts in London, or at his home in Aberdeen. We'd like to find him, and he's just a sample of a few hundred political hooligans with Scottish connections whom we regard as long shots but possible leads."

Gwynne-Vaughan frowned. What it all meant was that they had no real leads and were simply spreading the widest possible net in every area they could think of.

"Is there anything from Porton Down?"

"Nothing that helps. The security chief down there swears that none of their little phials of nerve gas have gone missing."

"It's the same story in West Germany and France. Max Brenner and Paul Cassin have already launched the thorough security checks that Steve Regan has requested. But every establishment that stocks nerve gas swears that its defenses are impregnable."

"So we come back to searching for the terrorist base. Was there any joy in your stopover in Oslo?"

"Full cooperation," Gwynne-Vaughan said. "They're alert to the possibility that our terrorists could be based on some isolated stretch of their own North Sea coastline, and they are laying on naval patrols of the unpopulated fiords, plus a low level air survey. However, I think they'll draw a blank. Like you I suspect that this particular terrorist group is operating somewhere in Scotland."

Nicolson stood up from his desk. An old bullet wound in his right leg gave him a cramp if he sat for too long. He moved stiffly to the window and stared out at the grey sky. His face was as cheerless as the weather.

"What really worries me, Sir Alexander, is that next time they might not be satisfied with an oil rig. They could just as easily launch a nerve gas attack over a town, or a city."

"They could," Gwynne-Vaughan agreed. "But they wouldn't get away so easily. Our offshore oil and gas rigs make very easy targets. Right now there are more than seventy production platforms and drilling rigs scattered over the North Sea, and it takes a navy patrol boat up to thirty-six hours to sail from the mouth of the Wash to north of the Shetlands. We've stepped up the air force patrols with long range Nimrods and Vulcans, but even so it's impossible to give every site round-the-clock protection."

Nicolson turned back to face him. "So you think they'll continue to attack the offshore oil industry."

"The rigs are vulnerable, and so far all the evidence points to a worldwide assault on non-Arab oil resources. I suppose that in the terms of their own twisted logic Terror Incorporated would argue that they are striking basically at capitalism, and not at people."

"But it's always people who suffer," Nicolson said

bitterly. "There were seventy-three men on those two oil rigs, plus the helicopter pilot who died, and the three men who were machine-gunned on the service ship. And as far as we know, it was only a beginning."

SIX

The brilliant blue and scarlet macaw sat calmly upon its perch with its heavy-beaked head tilted slightly to one side. The cage had been set down in the open on the bare, dusty earth, and through the bars the bird watched with one beady eye as the strangely dressed figure of a man moved around the helicopter. As well as protective clothing and gloves the man wore the face mask, harness and compressed air cylinder of a self-contained breathing apparatus. It was the type of set used by firemen to work in smoke, or when dealing with spillage from potentially dangerous chemicals.

Twenty yards further back Kanin Hisato and Yaeko Ishida also watched. They watched the bird as much as the man, for they did not wear protective clothing, and if the macaw should begin to flutter in panic then that would be their signal to run.

The man in the suit was Jiro Masaka. He disconnected the empty gas cylinder from the inlet to the crop-spraying tanks of the helicopter and carried it to one side. He laid it carefully beside the first cylinder he had emptied, straightened up, and then walked over to the cage. He lifted the cage and the macaw suddenly screamed.

Hisato and the girl tensed. For a second they were frozen but the bird's scream was merely one of indignation on being disturbed. It stretched its blue wings but then closed them again. The parrot beak also closed slowly and the bright eyes stared at Masaka as steadily as before. The macaw was still healthy, still gripping strongly to its perch with hooked claws, and they all relaxed.

Masaka lifted the cage and walked with it in a full circle around the helicopter. Then he opened the cabin door and put the cage on the pilot's seat. The bird looked puzzled by the performance but made no adverse reactions. Masaka was satisfied. He turned away more briskly, picked up the two empty gas bottles and moved them into the large wooden shed that served as a hangar for the helicopter. When he emerged he raised his gloved hands in smiling surrender and walked towards his two friends.

Hisato was holding a hose. Yaeko Ishida followed it back and turned on the tap valve. Masaka turned slowly and allowed Hisato to wash him down thoroughly with the jet of water.

Finally Masaka took the hose and walked back to wash down the helicopter. The macaw squawked with more noisy indignation when the water jet rattled over the curved perspex of the cockpit but Masaka was sufficiently confident now to ignore it. When he had finished the hosing down operation he stripped off his protective clothing.

"We are ready," he said calmly.

"But is it wise?" Hisato advocated a word of caution.

Yaeko Ishida flashed her black eyes upon him. She had already decided that today they would destroy another oil camp. She knew that Sharaf and Cobral had each accounted for two oil rigs on their first flight, and she was determined that her team would achieve no less. Hisato had already suggested that they wait, as the other teams were now doing, until the initial fuss and the upsurge of defense activity had died down. Ishida's answer was that the Amazon oil rigs were more widely

52

scattered and less easy to patrol than those of the Gulf of Mexico and the North Sea, and in any case she had nothing but contempt for the comic army and air force of Peru.

Now she looked at Hisato and there was scorn in her voice as she asked cruelly, "Are you afraid?"

Kanin Hisato was bare-chested. He wore only trousers and a sharp knife sheathed at his right hip. He stared at her for two seconds, and then the knife seemed to leap in a silver blur into his right hand. His left hand tore open his trousers to bare his belly below the naval. He reversed the blade of the knife and held it in front of him with two hands. His arms were stiff and the needle point was aimed at a spot one inch above the black pubic hairline. His raging eyes had not moved from her face.

"I think only of the overall success of our mission," he told her savagely. "I am not afraid of death. If you ask I will die now."

Yaeko knew that she had only to say the word and he would slam the blade home, rip up and twist and spill his intestines out at her feet. He would do it for honor, but his honor was a meaningless pride. Her only god was hate.

"Put away the knife," she commanded, and then she moved past him to remove the macaw and its cage from the helicopter.

Ten minutes later they were airborne with a horizon to horizon carpet of jungle green treetops passing below. They had an hour's flying time to their target, another American-owned oil drilling camp that was marked on their map as AmBase One. The sky was a ferocious, empty blue. Beneath the endless green waves of foliage were hidden, steaming depths that were the haunt of the deadly bushmaster and fer de lance. Down there was the insect and reptile-infested domain of the prowling jaguar. In the forest-smothered swamps and rivers swarmed the crocodiles and sting rays and the ravenous, flesh-eating piranha. The jungle concealed many horrors, but none with the hideous death potential of the lone metal bird that whirled serenely overhead.

During the sixty-minute flight they saw nothing of the Peruvian Air Force. Then Hisato lifted a hand from the controls and pointed ahead.

Yaeko leaned forward to watch as the break in the green wilderness below them gradually opened out into a large, manmade clearing. It was criss-crossed with the track marks of the giant bulldozers that had pushed back the undergrowth and the trees. To the west side of the clearing was the derrick with its powerful engines, pumps, mud tanks and the stacked piles of drill pipe. The central area had been left clear as a helicopter landing site, which meant that the crew huts, the cookhouse and the radio shack were all pressed up against the barrier of forest trees on the eastern side.

Yaeko looked down on the small, moving dots that were men working in the clearing and she bared her perfect white teeth. It was the smile of a she-wolf and her tongue flickered with sensual anticipation over her glistening lips.

The men below were Americans, the sons of the generation who had fought the Pacific War, and it was fitting that they should die in a writhing agony equal to the suffering of the victims of Nagasaki and Hiroshima. She thought of her father's burned and blistered face, and of her mother who was bald and blind, and she felt no pity for the Americans. All she felt was the terrible hatred that cried and cried aloud for vengeance.

Hisato glanced over his shoulder and she nodded her head in a violent motion that sent her black hair flying.

"Go down," she screamed at him. "Go down and let them taste death in all its sweetness."

Hisato pushed forward the control column, the whirling rotor blades tilted obediently in response and the helicopter swooped down over the oil camp.

The camp boss at AmBase One was a tall, tough, leather-faced Texan named John Marlowe. Except that no one ever called him John. He had been around in the oil industry for as long as anyone could remember, and he had always been "Mad Jack" to everyone who knew him. In a rough world that was full of horny and hard-hitting bastards, Mad Jack Marlowe was probably the horniest and hardest-hitting bastard of them all.

However, he hadn't got his reputation entirely from whoring and fighting and ripping oil out of the guts of the earth. When he wasn't doing any of those things Mad Jack liked to relax by taking risks. In the Arctic Circle he had hunted polar bears from a kayak. In Algeria he had hunted desert antelope and jackals from a racing jeep. In Sumatra he had hunted for tigers. Now the search for oil had dumped him in the Amazon and before he departed for the next location in the next God-forsaken back-of-beyond he intended to shoot a jaguar and the biggest anaconda he could find.

The rifle that Marlowe had carried all around the world over the past fifteen years was a US-made Garand, heavier and less fancy-looking than most modern hunting rifles, but reliable and accurate to 500 yards. It was an old and familiar friend and with it Marlowe knew that he could put a bullet practically anywhere he wanted. When it was not being used or oiled or merely handled the Garand hung on the wall above Marlowe's bunk.

When the helicopter made its first run Marlowe was sprawled on his bunk and snoring in a shallow sleep. He had worked a hard shift and handed over to his chief roustabout an hour before. He had eaten, swallowed three cans of beer and then decided to hit the sack for half an hour before he moved again. Then he planned to make a short foray into the forest and shoot a couple of monkeys for the cooking pot. His own men wouldn't eat them but the Indians who formed the menial labor force were quite partial to monkey meat.

The sound of the helicopter woke him up. He frowned because he wasn't expecting a chopper landing today, and in any case this particular chopper was not hovering but was already receding after the first sharp buzz of its passing. Then Marlowe remembered what had happened to AmBase Four on the upper reaches of the Maranon and a flash of instinct told him that the same thing was happening now. He sprang to his feet but the same instinct caused him to grab the Garand from the wall before he ran out into the open.

He was just in time to see the helicopter spinning away over the green treetops to the south. Then he looked to the rig and the drilling site on the far side of the clearing. He saw his men scattering in blind panic but they were running only for a few seconds. Then they began to stagger and fall. Some of them were screaming with all the power of their burning lungs, others just writhed and squirmed in the yellow mud as they choked into an excruciating eternity.

The handful of men who had emerged with Marlowe from the accommodation huts stared in soul-chilled horror. Then they turned and began to run desperately for the tangled depths of the jungle behind them.

Yaeko and Masaka looked back. They saw the men dying around the rig they had just sprayed with poison, and they also saw the men still standing alive on the opposite side of the camp. Yaeko gnashed her lovely teeth and clenched her tiny fists. She was afraid that the wind was unfavorable, blowing the gas from the rig area straight into the jungle instead of allowing it to drift across the wide clearing to the crew huts. The thought that some of the Americans might escape threw her into a frenzy and she shrieked again at Hisato.

"Turn back! Turn back and release the remainder of the gas."

Hisato turned the helicopter in a tight circle and headed back to the clearing. The sun was now directly ahead, causing all three Japanese to squint their narrowed eyes. As the oil camp appeared again Hisato saw the dead men still twitching around the base of the derrick and the drilling area. Then he saw the men running away from the buildings on the far side of the camp and disappearing into the jungle. He dipped the helicopter and swooped towards them.

Yaeko was leaning forward, her black eyes bright and her pink tongue licking slowly over red lips.

Masaka had his hand on the gas release lever.

Too late they all saw that one man was not running blindly away. Instead he was looking up at them and racing towards the helicopter with long, furious strides. He skidded to a stop and knelt abruptly. The long rifle in his hands was flung up to his shoulder as he aimed.

Simultaneously Hisato pulled back on the control column and Masaka opened the vents on the gas tanks.

Mad Jack Marlowe had the stock of the Garand pulled firmly against his shoulder. Already his throat was raw and burning and the tears from his eyes spilled down his leathery cheek and over the polished wood. The helicopter was a blur as it came down towards him and the roar of its engine and the thunder of the whirling blades was deafening.

He squeezed the trigger.

The perspex bubble of the cockpit vanished as the helicopter leaned back and climbed, presenting its underbelly with the last of the gas streaming invisibly from the open vents.

Marlowe's head was splitting open, he was coughing and crying and his chest was being crushed. With a blind effort of will he leaned back and jerked the Garand up.

57

He fired again.

The helicopter swept overhead with all the noise and force of a passing hurricane. The downrush of wind almost hammered him flat into the yellow mud. He was choking now, his whole nervous system crucified on a rack of pain. He was throwing up vomit as he twisted round on one knee, but incredibly the rifle was still grasped in his faltering hands.

The world went black. He was suffocating in his own private hell of pain and darkness. He couldn't see or think or act. All his senses and all his powers of coordination were washed out by the giant waves of indescribable agony. His body plunged forward, face-down and writhing, but the muzzle of the Garand was still pointed at the noise of the retreating helicopter.

As his elbow hit the ground his trigger finger contracted in one of a whole series of violent and uncontrollable muscle spasms and the Garand fired its final bullet.

Marlowe's first shot had punched a hole through the cabin perspex and then hit Kanin Hisato squarely between the eyes. The pilot fell back dead from the controls with the back of his head blown out. The helicopter had veered sideways, still climbing and the second shot had missed. Then Masaka and the girl had grabbed together for the control column. For a few seconds they fumbled it, the man cursing and the girl screaming. Then Yaeko had pulled back to let Masaka take over. He barely had time to level the machine before Marlowe's last, unaimed shot blasted into the fuel tank.

The helicopter exploded in mid-air in one almighty gout of scarlet flame. Wreathed in black oil smoke it plunged across the clearing like a flaming meteor, shedding its blades like great scythes before it crashed into the forest wall. The smaller trees snapped and splintered but the second ranks of one-hundred-year-old

58

giants merely shook and stood firm. The fireball of wreckage plummeted into the undergrowth.

Masaka died on impact but Yaeko Ishida remained alive for almost a minute. Trapped in her funeral pyre with the flames roaring around her she screeched wildly for help but no one came.

Mad Jack Marlowe had stopped moving and the clearing was full of dead men.

SEVEN

It was several hours before the murder of AmBase One was discovered by another helicopter pilot who was flying a mail delivery out from Iquitos. He hovered for a few seconds only before making a rapid climb and speeding back to his base. On the way he initiated the first of a frantic series of radio calls that flashed around the world.

From Iquitos, the oil base town on the Maranon, the news was relayed to Lima, the capital of Peru. There, by special pre-arrangement with the police and army, it was promptly telephoned to the US embassy. The powerful embassy transmitters sped it north to Washington, to the CIA headquarters at Langley, Virginia, and to Counter-Terror in New York. From there Roy Hanson relayed it south again to Galveston where Steve Regan and Wayne Johnson were still conducting the massive hunt for the light aircraft that had blotted out the Gulf oil rigs.

So far they had worked eighteen hours a day, mobilized more than twelve thousand law officers and turned over half of Texas, and they had learned nothing. However, Regan was not slow to recognize a break when it happened. He had top level contacts with both the air force and the CIA, plus a virtually blank check from the State Department, and he was not afraid to use them. When Regan started to move things moved with the speed of greased lightning.

He made a series of fast telephone calls. The first was to Freeman and by the time he had made the last the tall major had arrived with one of the silver protection suits they had worn to visit the offshore oil rig. Regan grabbed it with a brief word of thanks and left Johnson to explain. The New York Section Head for Counter-Terror was already making long-legged strides to the waiting police car that catapulted him along the super-highway to Houston.

It was night when the car arrived at Houston Airport with its siren howling and the red light flashing, and it was waved straight through on to the runway. An F-4 Phantom jet from the nearest air base had landed only minutes before and the pick-up took a matter of seconds. The copilot was standing on the runway, stripping off his flight suit and helmet. Regan put them on, zipped up and scrambled into the back seat. He had flown combat missions in Vietnam on his last duty tour with the air force and so the clothing and the machine were all familiar. The cockpit hood slammed down and the Phantom made a racing takeoff. The aircraft was fitted with long range fuel tanks for a straight through flight and they were on their way to Peru before Regan got round to the formality of saying hello to his pilot.

The Phantom landed at a Peruvian air force base on the western side of the Andes while the great ice peaks were still shrouded in darkness. Here the changeover was less smooth but nearly as fast and a lightweight Cessna U-3A made the last short hop to Iquitos. By then it was dawn, and looking down Regan saw a jungle-flanked river town that was more than half composed of water-borne shacks. Once Iquitos had been a rubber boom town. It had fallen into decay and disrepair but now it was taking up a new lease of life as the center of the mushrooming oil industry.

The Cessna landed and a reception committee was waiting.

Regan climbed out into a tangle of mostly Latin personalities and it took him ten minutes to sort out who was who and to get a coherent picture of what was happening. There was a noisy assortment of officials and a gaggle of police, army and air force officers who were trying to coordinate themselves with only a vague idea of what their forces might achieve. There was also a scattering of angry oil men. The only cool head in the immediate vicinity belonged to a crewcut young American named Galloway who had flown out from the US embassy in Lima.

Regan quickly realized that Galloway was a part of the local CIA, and also the man who was mainly responsible for smoothing his own fast and unimpeded progress through Peru. When there was a pause in the gabble of Latin voices it was Galloway who told him what he wanted to know.

"Nobody has yet made a ground-level visit to AmBase One," Galloway said. "They made that mistake when AmBase Four was wiped out and they lost a helicopter full of top brass."

"But there definitely is a crashed helicopter out there?"

Galloway nodded. "I talked to the pilot who started the alarm ball rolling. There's burned-out wreckage on the south side of the clearing and we know that there's no legitimate helicopter missing."

"I need to take a close-up look," Regan said grimly. "Find out which one of these medal-draped colonels is the air force boy and see if you can pull strings to borrow a helicopter for me."

It was an hour later, and less than twenty-four hours after the gas attack had first been discovered, when Steve Regan finally got his first glimpse of AmBase One. Encased in his silver suit he piloted the Peruvian air force helicopter in a slow circle over the large, silent clearing in the jungle. There was nothing alive down there, but he had expected nothing. He had done this before but it was no easier the second time around. He felt his guts crawl and his neck freeze.

Right now he would rather fly a Phantom into a hot dog fight with a couple of Mig 21s, or duck bullets in the battle-scarred streets of Beirut, or face up to any of the high-risk situations that had been packed into his active career. He was an action man who needed to move fast and fight, and nerve gas would never rate as his favorite enemy. Maybe it was okay for the bloodless, soulless Major Freemans of this world, but not for Steve Regan.

It had been a long, hectic night, and so far he had not even stopped for a cup of coffee. He was tired and his eyelids felt heavy, and for a moment he hesitated. Then he told himself that it couldn't be any worse than a moon walk and pushed the stick down.

He parked the helicopter in the center of the clearing and waited for the blades to stop and the dust to die down. Then he opened the door and got out slowly. He didn't want to make any rushed movements that might damage his suit.

He stood for a moment and looked round. Nothing moved. There was not even a breath of wind to move a leaf and the absolute stillness gave his stomach another slow churn. There were corpses littered everywhere around the oil camp, between the crew huts and around the rig, but Regan had no desire to examine any of them too closely. He knew that by now they would be rotting in the fierce heat, and stinking with their own released body waste. That made him doubly glad that he had his own self-contained air supply.

The sun was roasting him like a chicken wrapped up in silver foil and he could feel the sweat running down his body inside his suit. He looked ahead to the large, charred and blackened circle of jungle and began to walk towards it.

He had to step around two dead vultures, the first

carrion eaters who had dived upon the feast only to find that their meat was poisoned. Beyond the vultures the man on whom they had settled lay face down. Regan would have ignored him except that he saw the Garand rifle that had fallen within inches of the stiff, lifeless fingers.

The rifle muzzle was still pointed at the fire-blackened trees. Regan looked around more carefully and spotted two spent shells. He moved a dead vulture with his foot and saw the third. Now he was beginning to understand what had happened here.

There was nothing he could do for Mad Jack Marlowe and so he moved on.

The crashed helicopter had broken up on impact and several sections were scattered along the edge of the clearing. Regan picked his way around them to the twisted mass of skeletal framework which was all that was left of the cabin. Every step had to be made with great care, for he knew that if he ripped his suit on one of the many jagged edges of razor-sharp metal, or on one of the splintered branches of small trees that still thrust like charred and broken bones from the black earth, then he was a dead man.

He reached the wreckage of the cabin and looked inside. He counted three bodies burnt beyond recognition. Their own mothers would not have known them but it was still possible to make a reasonably accurate guess at their racial origin. One Regan assumed to be a woman. Her hair and clothes had been consumed by the flames but the shape of her breasts still showed. She had died with her eyes open. They were narrow, obviously Asian eyes. The bone structure of her forehead was flat, almost concave, and that suggested Japan more than any other part of Asia.

The Red Army of Japan was inevitably involved in every major terrorist crime and so Regan was not unduly surprised.

Regan stepped back and made a slow tour and examination of the rest of the wreckage. Most of the pieces were mangled and fire-ravaged but he found a central section of the long tail that had been thrown clear. The paint was badly blistered but it was still possible to read the last four figures and letters of the registration number. They were 500X. Regan searched for the next section of tail and finally found it high up in the branches of the surrounding trees. He had to change his position several times before he could make out another letter and a hyphen. The whole gave him I-500X.

He now had enough and he returned to his borrowed helicopter. He made a detour to avoid Marlowe and the vultures but then came to an abrupt stop as he almost set his foot upon a half-coiled bushmaster with its jaws open to bare needle-sharp fangs. The sweat turned to a coating of ice along his spine but the snake was dead like everything else. It had met with a venom more deadly than its own.

Regan swallowed hard and then hurried the last few steps. He didn't relax until he was airborne again, and then he had to breathe deeply a few times and wet his lips before he switched on his radio to report to Iquitos airport control.

Tracing the registration number I-500X was only a matter of time. It had been issued by the Peru air traffic licensing authority to a private pilot named Felipe Bozzanos. The name was known to the Iquitos Police Chief and most of the airport officials and excited a virulent gabble of Spanish. Galloway translated to inform Regan that Bozzanos operated from a small field a few miles to the north. He was a civilian pilot who had bought an ex-air force machine cheap and set himself up in the crop-spraying business with the big landowners further west. A year ago he had moved down into the Amazon where the oil industry had promised rich pickings for a freelance helicopter pilot. Lately he hadn't made any known flights for any of the oil companies and so it was reasonable to assume that he had found something that was still more lucrative.

"Let's go and see what we can wring out of him," Regan said grimly.

He had to throw away his half-finished cup of coffee in order to lead the stampede.

Felipe Bozzanos was stretched out comfortably in a hammock that was slung across the verandah of the raised wooden shack that was his home. He was snoring happily in a very drunken sleep with the neck of an empty rum bottle still clutched to his chest. He had spent most of the last three months in that blissfully comatose state and he didn't even hear the descending thunder of police jeeps and army trucks that stormed his airfield as though they had come to open up World War Three. However, he did wake when the police chief tipped up the hammock with an angry heave and dropped him with a crash on the hard boards. For good measure every boot that was within reach kicked out and rolled him violently across the verandah.

Felipe Bozzanos then endured the roughest ten minutes of his life. He was a little fat man who made an excellent punchball and he was hurled about the verandah like a mouse that had been suddenly pounced upon by a gang of sadistic predator cats. He barely knew what was happening and only managed to answer one of the shrieking flood of angry questions. He didn't know where his helicopter was or what it was being used for.

"All right, give him a break!" Regan pushed into the middle of the mob and let out a bellow. The attacking circle of dark Spanish faces hesitated and stared at him in surprise. "Sober him up," Regan finished. "Douse him with cold water and pour some black coffee down his throat. Then ask the questions."

Galloway swiftly translated into Spanish for those who had not understood. There were a few expressions of disappointment but on the whole the senior interrogators nodded reluctant agreement. An army sergeant found a hose reel attached to a tap at the side of the building and brought it on to the verandah with a grin of triumph. Seconds later Bozzanos was coughing and spluttering under the stinging impact of the first shower he had taken in weeks.

When Regan was satisfied that he could turn his back without the South American pilot being beaten to death he drew Galloway to one side.

"It's going to take time to get this guy sober," Regan said softly. "So maybe a couple of us cowboys can take a quiet look around while the rest of the posse is still busy."

Galloway nodded and they moved quietly into the building. In the first room there was a table with a scrap of dirty plastic cloth, two chairs, a sink full of unwashed plates and cups and an indescribably ancient and filthy electric cooker. On the walls were a couple of outdated calendars and hanging from a nail a dead squirrel monkey that had been stripped and cleaned ready for the pot. Flies buzzed around the latter and Galloway wrinkled his nose in distaste.

There was only one cupboard which Regan briefly opened. It contained tins, scraps of food, and a dozen full bottles of rum. They had already noticed the pile of empty bottles beside the verandah which meant that someone had kept Bozzanos well supplied with his favorite booze.

They moved into the bedroom. Here there was a rumpled bed with dirty sheets, a chest of drawers and a wardrobe. A few magazine pictures of female film stars were stuck to the walls and on the dressing table was a full ashtray and an old radio. Regan pulled open the drawers and turned over the mainly grey items of clothing inside. He found nothing more interesting than a collection of greasy, much handled pornographic pictures.

Galloway checked the wardrobe. Inside was a poncho, a jacket, a pair of boots and a stack of cheap magazines. Together they turned over the mattress and bedclothes. Beneath the bed was a full chamber pot that stank, and again Galloway registered disgust.

They became aware of the police chief standing in the doorway. He had watched them without comment. Regan shrugged. The police chief shrugged in return and gazed up at the ceiling. He saw nothing there and looked down again. He stared at the chamber pot which the two Americans had left untouched and then looked closer. He also had no intention of soiling his own hands but he shouted for one of his aides.

"Lazy dogs usually piss over the edge of the verandah," Galloway translated for Regan after the chamber pot had been carried out and emptied on to the dusty earth outside. An oilskin package had been tipped out and a police sergeant opened it up to reveal a double stack of large denomination Peruvian banknotes.

"About thirty thousand dollars worth," Galloway added when the pile had been counted. "That's more than Bozzanos could expect to earn in a year of regular flying out here, so I guess it's what they paid him for the use of his helicopter."

Regan nodded agreement and looked around the small field.

There were only two other buildings, one obviously a hangar and the other a long shack with a verandah similar to the one they had just explored.

"The Japs probably slept over there," Regan guessed.

They walked over and again the beaming police chief kept them company. It took only a few minutes to inspect the second hut and it was immediately obvious that it had been used by the Japanese. It was much cleaner than the hut of their South American host. The table had been cut down to a height of eighteen inches and three neatly arranged cushions showed that they had followed the usual Japanese custom of sitting on the floor. They had cooked on brand new camping gas equipment and every utensil gleamed spotlessly. In the bedroom there were no beds, just three mattresses and three sleeping bags rolled up and stacked against the wall. Clean straw mats covered the bare boards of the floor.

There were also three large, fully-packed rucksacks, as though the owners lived ready to depart at a moment's notice. Galloway took one, Regan another, and the police chief the third. They turned out clothing, a few books and toilet articles. Galloway's pack yielded the feminine things and ultimately a large scale map of South America.

They opened the map up on the floor and saw that it was peppered with black crosses. Each one, Regan realized, marked the site of an oil camp, a tank farm or some other type of oil installation. All the existing and proposed oil pipelines had been carefully drawn in and every oil port was heavily underlined. In addition the two crosses that marked AmBase One and AmBase Four had been circled with red ink.

As if they needed any more the army major came to tell them that his men had discovered a protection suit, breathing apparatus, and four empty and two full gas cylinders in the hangar.

"Let's go back and talk to Bozzanos," Regan decided grimly.

When he was capable Felipe Bozzanos talked. He was a soaking wet, trembling, coffee-scalded wreck of a man, and when it penetrated into his aching, rum-sodden brain that his helicopter had crashed and the Japanese were all dead he saw no choice but to tell all. The story was worked out of him with repeated cuffs and kicks and finally Galloway was able to put it together.

A year ago Bozzanos had been approached by a man and a woman who had offered to hire his helicopter for a very generous cash payment. Their only terms were that they would supply their own pilots. Bozzanos, whose only dream in life was one of easy money and free booze, had quickly succumbed to temptation. The strangers had made a down payment as a gesture of good faith and gave him instructions to move his base down to Iquitos and wait. Bozzanos had obeyed and flown a few jobs for the oil companies to set up his cover. Then the girl had returned two months before with the three Japanese and more money. After that Bozzanos had taken life easy and let them get on with it. His dream had come true and he neither knew nor cared about what happened next.

"Ask him about the man and the girl who set this up," Regan said. "I want their names, or at least some descriptions."

Galloway translated into Spanish and the police chief and his assistants added emphasis in their customary crude manner. Bozzanos flinched under the blows and gabbled some more.

"He doesn't know their names," Galloway said at last. "Except that the girl was called Julia. They were both South Americans but he doesn't think that they lived in Peru. They spoke Spanish but they used some words that are not common here. The girl had black hair and was about thirty-three. The man was older but still handsome." Galloway paused and then interpreted the next bit with a comic grimace. "Apparently he had a large cobra tattooed on his chest."

"Tell him to keep thinking. These two are important. Without them the trail ends here and every detail helps."

Galloway nodded and spoke again in Spanish. Bozzanos collected a few more bruises from the local law and moaned something that sounded like a plea for mercy. The police chief and his aides stopped suddenly and stared at their victim. Galloway turned an excited face to Regan.

"He says why do we keep beating him? Why don't we go and punish the girl?"

"You mean she's here?"

Bozzanos looked at him hopefully and mumbled through his split lips.

"Staying in a hotel in Iquitos," Galloway almost shouted. "He doesn't know which one, but she's definitely still around and monitoring the Japanese."

"Let's move," Regan rapped. And Bozzanos was temporarily reprieved.

There was not exactly an abundance of hotels in Iquitos and most of them catered to short-stopover tourists or established oil men. The one hotel that had accommodated a solo young woman over the past two months was not difficult to locate but they arrived too late. The girl, who had been registered under the name of Julia Herrero, had checked out and departed on a plane for Lima the previous day. Thinking back the hotel manager remembered that she had packed in a hurry soon after Iquitos had been flooded with the first rumours concerning the events at AmBase One.

Regan and Galloway caught the next flight to Lima. Galloway had telephoned ahead and on arrival they learned that Julia Herrero was still one jump ahead on an international flight to Caracas.

"It figures," Regan said with conviction. "There were a number of guerrilla attacks on land oil installations in Venezuela to coincide with the nerve gas attacks on the oil rigs, so we know there is a Venezuelan link."

EIGHT

The sun was burning high over the arid Texas landscape when the white patrol car carrying the silver insignia of the sheriff's office pulled up on the state highway a hundred miles southwest of Galveston. Deputy Sheriff Dan Parker leaned back from the wheel and shifted the well-chewed wad of spearmint gum from the left to the right side of his rhythmically moving jaws as he gazed up at the board sign that read: KASLER AIRFIELD, PRIVATE.

This would make the eleventh call that Parker had personally made on private airfields in the area over the past few days and he was glad that it was the last. Texas was a big, rich state, and it seemed that every other guy in it had enough cash and enough need to own a private airplane. Parker figured that a deputy sheriff in this particular county had enough to do in the normal line of business without all this extra drag-assing around, but he decided he'd better get on with it anyway.

He turned the patrol car off the highway and up the dirt track.

When he reached the airfield there was no sign of life and no sign of a plane. He drove up to the ranch house, stopped and switched off his engine. He got out of the car and stretched. He was a long, rangy man with an appetite like a horse, but he never put on weight. He saw the ranch house door opening and carefully ejected his wad of gum with a sideways spit. He chewed to relax while driving, but he didn't like to give the impression that every county sheriff was a gum-chewing hick.

Frank Kasler walked to meet him, looking nervous.

"Morning, Frank." They had downed a few beers together at one of the bars in town so Parker saw no need to be formal.

"Morning, Dan—" Kasler was looking at Parker's badge and gunbelt as though they scared him. "What brings you out here?"

"Bullshit, I guess." Parker leaned his rump comfortably against the door of his car. "I've got a pile of questions I'm supposed to ask every guy who owns an airplane, so I reckon that has to include you."

"What's it about?"

"Gawd knows. Maybe the big chiefs know too, but they don't tell us Injuns everything. Maybe somebody's been doing something with an airplane that he shouldn't." He grinned and his eyes became quizzical. "You been doing anything illegal with your plane, Frank?"

Kasler could feel panic inside but he forced an answering grin. "Not that I know of."

"You made any flights lately?"

"Not for the past month."

"Uh-huh, how about last Friday to be exact? Did you make any flights on Friday, Frank?"

"Hell, I told you, my plane hasn't left the ground in the last month." There was tension in his voice and Kasler hoped that Parker wasn't smart enough to know it.

"Don't get sore now." The rangy sheriff held up his hands in mock defense. "That's just one of the questions I'm supposed to ask."

There was a moment of silence. Parker scratched gently at his paw. Kasler stood uncomfortable. Parker looked at Kasler again.

"A month, Frank? Is business that slack?"

74

"It's a slack time of year."

"So what's the last flight you made?"

Kasler had to think back. "I did some crop-spraying for Pete Edmonds over at his place."

"Uh-huh," Parker looked thoughtful. "I talked to Hank Judd yesterday. He told me that he did some crop-spraying at the Edmonds ranch last week. How come you lost the job? You have some kind of a bust-up with Pete?"

Kasler's mouth was dry and he badly needed a drink.

"I got the offer," he said, "but I had to turn it down. I had the engine stripped. The magneto was buggered."

"Well, that about wraps it up." Parker pushed himself away from the car. Then he paused. "Except that I have to take a look at your airplane."

"What for?" Kasler almost choked over the two words.

"Hell, it's just another of those things I'm *supposed* to do. I have to check your flight log for one thing. You do keep a flight log? And you do keep it in the airplane?"

Kasler nodded. He could feel a crawling itch between his shoulder blades and he knew that was where the muzzle of the machine pistol was pointed. He prayed to God that they could hear clearly what was happening and would realize that he didn't have any choice.

"Let's go then," Parker said as though he wanted to get it over and get home. He strolled towards the hangar and Kasler followed, flinching, at his heels.

When the hangar was opened up they moved inside. The red and silver Piper Cherokee was still parked in the dead center but Kasler noticed that now the line of silver cylinders against the wall had been covered with a piece of old tarpaulin. Parker walked around the plane as though he had never seen one before. He stopped under the nose and looked up.

"She sure looks all right to me, Frank."

"I fixed it," Kasler said. "It wasn't a big job." He stood by the door and was reluctant to come closer.

Parker looked back at him, his lean, thoughtful face shadowed in the gloom. "Uh-huh," he mused slowly. Then as though satisfied, "How about finding that log book for me?"

Kasler's mouth twitched. He would sooner have gone into a cage full of starving cougars than approach the plane, but he couldn't afford to let Parker know that. His legs didn't want to move but he made a supreme effort and walked forward. He was gritting his teeth and he didn't dare to look Parker in the face as he passed.

Touching the plane took another effort of will and his sweating hand slipped off the door handle as he pulled it down. The door swung open and he reached in to pull the log book out of the deep pocket inside the door. He walked away with it quickly, back to the open hangar door where there was a wide shaft of sunlight.

Parker followed him and he handed over the log book. Parker's lean face showed no expression as he turned over the pages, and Kasler hoped that Parker would think that he had moved away just to bring the book into the light.

"It checks," Parker said after he had read the last entry. "Three hours crop spraying at the Edmonds ranch, fourteenth of August this year, that's a month ago." He looked up and handed the book back.

Once to the plane was enough. Kasler didn't want to return the log book. He stood with it in his hands and Parker looked at him curiously. Then the deputy sheriff glanced back to the plane, his gaze taking in the control dials visible through the open door.

Christ, Kasler thought, if he checks the mileage then he'll know she's made a flight since the last entry. The sweat oozed out of him and his stomach felt like melting jelly. A gallon of liquor now wouldn't have been enough.

"One more thing, Frank——"

76

Parker started but didn't finish because Gloria Kasler appeared in the open doorway. She interrupted quickly:

"Frank, there's a telephone call for you up at the ranch house."

"For me?" Kasler spoke weakly and knew he sounded stupid. The reprieve had him bewildered.

"Sure," Gloria nodded. "The man says it's urgent and it sounds like a job. You haven't had a job in the last month and we need some eating money. You'd best see to it."

Kasler looked at Parker. "You excuse me, Dan?"

Parker grinned amiably. "I was about through anyway, and we all have to eat."

"I can stay and talk to Sheriff Parker," Gloria smiled sweetly at one man and the sharp flicker of her eyes told the other to get up to the house.

Kasler made a gesture of acknowledgement to Parker and then hurried away. The log book was still clenched in his fist.

When her husband had gone Gloria switched on her smile again. Her blonde hair was combed loose and she wore very brief white shorts and a sun top that flaunted a very sexy body. She knew she looked good even if her style was brazen.

"What's this visit all about, Sheriff?"

"Oh, just a pack of damfool questions that I'm supposed to ask."

"Why ask Frank?"

"Not just Frank, especially, but any guy who owns an airplane."

"Well, if there's anything I can tell you—" Her eyes hinted at something else. "Or do for you?"

"Not just now. I reckon Frank's given me all the answers I need."

Gloria smiled. Her hands were resting casually on her thighs and she moved them lightly over the bare flesh. She knew that trick had the knack of starting the heavy breathing in an observant male.

"You sure it's only answers you need, Sheriff?"

Parker looked her up and down. "This time maybe." He was carefully vague.

Gloria still smiled. She turned away and moved out of the hangar. Her buttocks rolled smoothly beneath the tight shorts as she walked. Parker strolled after her and they both glanced towards the ranch house where Kasler was disappearing through the door.

"I think Frank is going to be tied up for some time," Gloria predicted. "These business calls get pretty long-winded." She gave him a speculative glance. "If you do need to talk to Frank some more you can come up to the house. I'll fix us a drink while you wait."

"Well, thank you, Ma'am." Parker looked reluctantly at his wristwatch. "But I've got all I need and I've got other things to do. Maybe some other time."

"Some other time," Gloria repeated, and her eyes sparkled with promises.

She walked with him back to his car and waved him a cheerful goodbye.

When he was out of sight Parker broke open another pack of spearmint gum and slipped a stick between his teeth. He relaxed at the wheel as he began to chew, his eyes squinting at the dirt track ahead. He wondered if they really believed that a Texas drawl made a county sheriff into some kind of a dumb mulehead.

Two hours later Dan Parker was in the County Sheriff's office talking to Wayne Johnson. The Deputy Section Head for Counter-Terror had moved up fast from Galveston and he was listening intently to every word that Parker had to say.

"You're sure that this man Kasler was scared?" Johnson said.

"Sure I'm sure." Parker nodded soberly. "He would have looked happier if I had been a rattlesnake sitting on his breakfast table. When I asked him if I could see the plane he looked so bad I thought for a minute the plane wasn't there. Then I figured he was scared of the plane itself. He acted like it was diseased."

"Did you ask him if anyone had approached him with an offer for using his plane?"

"I was supposed to, but his wife kinda horned in before I could get around to it. If I had, or if I'd asked him if he'd flown over any oil rigs lately, then I reckon he just might have shit hisself."

"What was the make and coloring of the plane?"

"It was a Piper Cherokee, red and silver."

"It fits," Johnson said with conviction. "There was a red and silver light aircraft spotted over the Gulf coast on the day the oil rigs were attacked. We haven't traced it yet but the sighting would be in a direct line between here and the rigs.

"Red and silver, red and white, they're popular colors for small aircraft." Parker made the comment then dismissed it. "But I still figure you're right."

"Tell me about the Kaslers."

"Well, Frank Kasler drinks far too much, and there's talk around town that Gloria is an easy lay. I wouldn't know, even though she was definitely acting it up to steer me away from Frank. Maybe she's just one of these women who looks like an easy lay, if you know what I mean."

Johnson didn't answer so Parker shrugged and went on: "Anyway, Frank flies crop-spraying for the local ranchers. About a year ago he crashed his plane and damned near killed himself. He was lucky someone dragged him out of it and the plane burned up. Frank was flying drunk at the time and he was fool enough to have forgotten to pay up his insurance cover. He wound up dead broke, really busted!"

"But now he's got another plane?"

Parker nodded. "Frank spent eight months drowning his sorrows. It looked like Gloria was fixing to leave him and he was just going to drink his way deeper into the trash heap. Then out of the blue he acquires another plane."

"Just like that?" Johnson said skeptically.

"Just like that." Parker shrugged again. "There was no major unsolved crime in the territory. Nobody had just heisted a payroll or busted a bank, so we have to assume that it was legal. Somebody could have died and left him the money."

"That's not good enough any more," Johnson decided flatly. "It's high time we found out exactly where Frank Kasler did raise the cash to buy that new airplane."

"Another visit?"

"Not by you, Sheriff. If there is a terrorist group manipulating the Kaslers then we've got to do some pretty careful thinking before we make our next move.

The big Negro reached for the telephone to call up Houston, Galveston and New York. He was going to need some specialized help drafted into this area fast and he could make plans after he had got things moving.

NINE

When Steve Regan came out of the passenger reception concourse at Venezuela's Maiquetia International Airport he found a polished white Pontiac convertible waiting. A miniature flag of the USA fluttered from the tiny mast on the hood and a slim-built man with black, curly hair was sitting at the wheel. He leaned across the car and pushed open the passenger door.

"Hi there, Hotshot!" The white grin in the dark face was a huge, warm welcome. "Climb in and tell an old buddy what's new with the superspy business."

Regan had snatched a few hours sleep on the flight but not enough, but now his rough-hewn face cracked into a smile. Joe Minnelli was an old CIA friend he hadn't seen since Tokyo and that was five years back.

"Didn't you know I quit? I'm a kind of superpoliceman now." Regan slid into the car and gripped Minnelli's hand hard. "Hi, Joe. It's good to see you."

"You too, Steve." Once Regan had put a fast bullet into a communist agent who had been close to sticking Minnelli with a knife and Minnelli had not forgotten. However, you didn't embarrass a guy who had saved your life and the Hotshot nickname was enough reminder. Minnelli started the car and headed it smoothly to the main highway.

"Caracas is a twenty minute drive," he promised.

Regan settled back to enjoy it. They were three thousand feet above sea level and the modern white-block city ahead was sited in a rift valley enclosed on the north and south by the towering mountain ranges of the central highlands of Venezuela. It was dramatic scenery but after a minute he glanced again at Minnelli.

"You're a surprise, Joe. When did they shift you out here?"

Minnelli gave a shrug and a grin. "You know how it goes, Steve. Back in Tokyo we had one of those scandals the local press loves to blow up out of all proportion. Somebody goofed and the Korean ambassador found a bug in his telephone. Naturally the CIA got the blame, and because it was time for me to be moved on anyway, I got elected as the fall guy. My predecessor out here had got himself assassinated one dark night so there was a convenient vacancy. So, here I am."

"How's Maria?"

"Fine, how's Lydia?"

"Better than I deserve." Regan smiled wearily. "Staying faithful to me makes her one in a million. This makes the third time this year I've had to shoot off half way around the world without even saying goodbye."

They talked over old times in Tokyo until they reached the embassy. They entered by a side door and adjourned to a small suite of offices through a door that bore the gold-lettered words: AIR ATTACHE. MAJOR J. A. MINNELLI. Inside Minnelli broke open a bottle of bourbon and outwardly they relaxed. Minnelli sat down behind his desk and pulled loose his tie. Regan sat down in the spare chair and did the same. They both drank bourbon.

"Business?" Minnelli finally asked.

Regan nodded. "Julia Herrero. How much did you find out?"

"Nothing too exciting, but the lady's name does show up on our files. She's thirty-three years old, unmarried, has communist and pro-Castro student friends and sympathies, and she works as a secretary for a private language school. It's run by a man named Cobral who teaches English to Venezuelan students, and Spanish to Americans and Europeans intending to take up residence here in Caracas."

"If she's that unexciting, why is she on file?"

"Mainly because of her connection with this man Cobral. He's a strong, left-wing intellectual. As a young man he preached communism and armed revolution as the only alternative to the Jiminez dictatorship. For that the secret police threw him into jail along with a few thousand other political prisoners whom they locked up and tortured. If you know your Latin American history, Steve, then you'll know that Jiminez was one of the last and one of the worst of the old-style South American dictators. He ruled Venezuela for seven years. He closed down the university, muzzled the press, stamped down on everybody and made himself and his pals rich out of the oil revenues. Any opponent who escaped his jails went underground, into the hills or into exile."

"As I remember it he got toppled in fifty-seven," Regan said. "The army, the navy, and the air force all got together and threw him out."

"That's right." Minnelli nodded. "Jiminez had the gall to hold elections with himself as the only candidate. All the others he had arrested. It seems that up till then you could dictate to Venezuelans but you couldn't insult their intelligence. There were mass riots in Caracas that led to over three hundred people being slaughtered by the Jiminez police. At that point the armed forces had to step in."

"And Cobral was still in jail?"

"He was, but after Jiminez was overthrown most of the political prisoners were released, including Cobral."

"What's his record since then?"

"Low profile. He's been hauled in for questioning a couple of times by the police, but each time he's been released again with nothing proven. There were obviously several very clever and determined minds behind the wave of terrorist acts that occurred in the early nineteen-sixties, but they were never caught. Luis Cobral could have been one of them, some people think he was, but nobody really knows."

"You're losing me, Joe. You'd better fill me in with some more background."

"Okay. Since Jiminez, Venezuela has had democratically elected governments, but up until the late nineteen-sixties they were still plagued with extremist guerrilla groups, both left and right wing. Under Jiminez these groups all had to go underground and resort to jungle warfare and terrorism. I guess they developed a guerrilla mentality and they just carried on their power struggle. The communists of course got an extra boost when Castro won Cuba in sixty-two, and he gave them help to try and repeat the process here. The oil revenues were fluctuating and caused a lot of dissatisfaction which gave them all something to exploit."

"And they had faith in the philosophy of revolution through terror," Regan guessed shrewdly.

Again Minnelli nodded. "The armed forces had proved their strength, and there were mutinies at a couple of naval bases where some of the younger officers wanted to carry it all a few steps further to the left. Both were crushed pronto, and a number of young captains and lieutenants fled to the hills to join the guerrillas. At that time half the states in Venezuela had a guerrilla problem on twenty different fronts. They formed an army of liberation, the FALN. Then we had acts of piracy, the first skyjackings, the sabotage of oil installations and more riots. Some of the incidents were really spectacular."

"Which means that somebody had already appreciated the publicity value of terrorism."

"Sure, the PLO and your Jap terrorists could have learned a lot in Venezuela."

"Perhaps they did," Regan said grimly. "But finish the briefing, Joe. I've got a hunch this background you're filling in could be important. Obviously the terror campaign failed."

"For a number of reasons," Minnelli agreed. "First the FALN had set up a man named Ojeda as their president. He was the national figure who led the junta that overthrew the Jiminez regime. That ensured them a lot of popular support, but when Ojeda was assassinated by a right wing group they had no one to replace him. Then the FALN blundered badly with their Kill-A-Cop-A-Day campaign. They kept it up for five hundred days, but most Venezuelan policemen come from large, low strata families. Five hundred murdered cops left a hell of a lot of grieving relatives and friends, and public opinion turned right against the FALN."

Minnelli paused to finish his drink before he continued: "The final blow came when the FALN tried to invade Venezuela from an offshore island they had set up with Castro's help as a training base. A couple of B52 bombers dropped hot steel shit on the landing parties and scattered them to hell and back. Since then the guerrillas have been quiet. The democratic process has held good, and all the elected presidents have served out their full terms of office."

"The guerrillas have been quiet until last Friday," Regan corrected. "Then they hit three oil targets, a tank farm, a refinery, and a drilling rig on Lake Maracaibo. Do you figure it's the work of an entirely new group, or one of the old groups starting up again."

"It's more likely to be one of the old groups. Some of them are still alive and kicking out there in the jungles." Minnelli looked at him doubtfully. "But you think that these new attacks are all tied in with the dead rigs off the Texas coast, on the Amazon and the North Sea?"

Regan nodded affirmative and then gave Minnelli a return briefing. "The fact that Julia Herrero was involved with the Japanese terror squad in Iquitos leads us straight back to Cobral," he finished. "The background you've just described sounded an ideal environment for breeding new recruits for Terror Incorporated. That makes this man Cobral very interesting. I want to know more."

Minnelli frowned and thought for a minute. "There's not much more to tell, Steve. For the past ten years Luis Cobral has outwardly done nothing more sinister than run his English-Spanish language school, with himself as the only tutor. Suspicion falls upon him mainly through association. One of the young naval officers involved in the anti-government mutinies, a man named Vincenzi who later became a guerrilla leader, spent several months studying English at the school. Several young women who attended Cobral's classes also became revolutionaries or rioters, or they influenced their brothers or lovers to go the same way. Cobral has quite a reputation as a seducer. And it looks as though he may have taught a lot more than just Spanish and English."

"Like sex, and a seminar on terrorism."

"That's possible. We know that the Venezuelan secret police made at least one attempt to slip a girl spy into the school. But she didn't act her part well enough in the bedroom or in the classroom. Cobral is either innocent or he smelled a rat. He didn't give her any lectures on terrorism."

"I smell a rat now," Regan said. "Where can I find him?"

"The language school is on the Avenida Margarita. Cobral has an apartment above the premises, but he's not there now. I sent a man round to check as soon as your information request on Julia Herrero came through. The language school has been closed for the past month and nobody in the building has seen anything of Cobral during that time. I'm trying to find out more, but for all I know at this moment he could be up in the hills or out of the country."

"What about the girl? Is she still in Caracas?"

"She has her own apartment on the Calle De Fernandez, number 87B. It's on the third floor. That's where she went after she got off the plane from Lima. I've got a discreet tail on her so I know she's still there."

"She's my next call," Regan said. "I think it's time I took some lessons in Spanish."

Caracas was practically an all-modern city, dominated by the twin thirty-two story towers of the Centro Simon Bolivar which Regan passed on his way to the Calle De Fernandez. His taxi took him through the Plaza Bolivar, flanked by the Palace of Justice, City Hall and the Cathedral. Very few of the new central buildings dated back more than a decade, but when the taxi stopped they were in the old part of the city where narrow streets cut up the square blocks. Regan paid off the *mestizo* driver and got out on to the pavement.

It was mid-afternoon and hot. The Calle De Fernandez was dusty and near deserted. Most of the shops had closed for siesta. Regan went into number 87 and up the staircase to the third floor. He pressed the bell beside the door marked 87B.

It was a few minutes before Julia Herrero came to the door. She was tall with olive-skinned Indian features and long, gleaming black hair. She wore a tight-fitting black dress that was cut almost like a uniform, emphasizing her curves but making them untouchable. She was beautiful, if you liked that kind of girl, but her eyes were cold.

"Señor?" Her tone coated the word with several degrees of frost.

Regan smiled at her. He had found time to shave and buy a clean shirt and hoped that he looked presentable. He knew that he wasn't young enough or hairy enough to pose as a student so he had decided on another approach.

"Miss Herrero, my name is Regan. I'm an executive with Occidental Oil and I'm going to be working in Caracas for a year. I need to know Spanish and I've been recommended the Cobral School of Languages."

"The school is closed." Julia Herrero said flatly.

"I know." Regan tried to look apologetic. "I called there this afternoon. I was told by the caretaker in the building that you work for Señor Cobral. Perhaps you can tell me when he will return? Or when I can enroll for the next course of Spanish lessons?"

"Señor Cobral is on a long vacation. I suggest you find another language school."

"I don't want to waste time with a second-rate teacher. I want the best and Señor Cobral was recommended."

"I am sorry. The school will be closed for at least a month."

She started to close the door but Regan didn't back off.

"Maybe you could teach me," he suggested. "I understand that you do work with Señor Cobral, and I need a crash-course in Spanish in a hurry."

"I am a secretary, not a teacher."

There was no encouragement. Regan knew that his last card was a loser but he played it anyway.

"You don't have to teach in a classroom. We could mix business with pleasure. Tonight I could take you out to dinner."

"Señor Regan." She stared at him without blinking. "I am what you call a lesbian. With me you would get no pleasure."

"That makes you a challenge." Regan tried a grin but it failed.

"Goodbye, Señor Regan," Julia Herrero said icily.

Then she pushed the door shut in his face.

Later Regan conferred again with Minnelli.

"They're attacking oil," he said. "But the prospect of milking an oil executive of anything he might know didn't tempt her. And she tried the butch routine to freeze me off. I think she's scared, Joe. But she's hard and sharp and there's no quick and easy way of cracking her open to get at what she knows. We can't prove that she's ever committed any crime here in Venezuela, so it looks as though she intends to sit tight and say nothing."

"In this part of the world the police don't always need proof before they take action," Minnelli said thoughtfully. "If I leak the facts into the right ear she could be pulled in for questioning. Or I could tip off the police *and* arrange for the girl to get a few minutes warning before they move in. That way we could panic her into running, and then watch to see where she runs to."

Regan considered both ideas but he didn't feel that either was satisfactory. "This girl's an Arctic clam. She won't talk unless they use torture and then there could be one hell of a political stink if it ever got out that we were involved. Making her run is the better idea. The odds are good that she will lead us to the local guerrilla group who caused the three explosions on Friday so it's worth a try. The snag is that she's smart enough to spend a couple of months making detours before she gets there, and I need a short cut direct to Cobral. I've still got two terror teams armed with that goddamned nerve gas loose somewhere in Texas and England. They have to be my number one priority."

"So what kind of a short cut do you have in mind?"

"There's only one, the language school on the Avenida Margarita. If it was a school for terrorists then there should be some evidence, documents, diagrams, perhaps even maps. A register of students could give us a more flexible lead than the glacial Señorita Herrero!"

"I've never done a burglary in my life," Minnelli said wryly. "But since Watergate we're all supposed to be experts. It can be arranged."

TEN

Detective Sergeant Derek Burnett stood formally in front of Mark Nicolson's desk in the Counter-Terror office at New Scotland Yard. He was a clean-looking young officer who was almost too respectful for a CID man, but he had a sharp memory for everything he saw or heard. Put him with a loudmouth to do the actual bullying, Nicolson thought, and you would have the basis for a very good investigating team.

"That *Sunday Times* article on VX nerve gas was published on the first of January," Burnett said quietly. He had his official police notebook in his hand but he didn't need to refer to it. "On Monday the second of January the London Patent Office did receive several visitors. The office keeps a visitor's book and I have a list of their names here."

He paused, and then went on with slight emphasis. "The interesting one is a girl who spent most of the morning in the section where the VX formula was temporarily filed. An attendant remembers that she claimed to be a student doing a research paper on insecticides. He helped her to find the patent specifications to some relatively harmless stuff and left her to write up her notes. She didn't ask for the VX patent but she did have the opportunity to look it up. The *Times* article showed a picture of the head of the patent document. It gave the application number, the international classification number, and the Patent Office index number at acceptance. It was all made very easy for her."

"Too bloody easy," Nicolson said sourly. He glanced at the photostat copy of the offending columns of newsprint that lay on his desk and inwardly he shivered. One mistake by the Defense Department, another by a national newspaper, and all hell could be let loose. It was a frightening world. He looked back to Burnett and asked, "What name did she give?"

"She signed the book as Fiona Smith, but the attendant who helped her thinks that she may have had a Scottish accent."

"What else does he remember?"

"Nothing really, sir. He thinks she might have had black hair but it was a long time ago."

"Long enough to go into production and manufacture a small stockpile of the stuff," Nicolson said bitterly. "The *Times* even makes a point of explaining that any chemistry student with a little ingenuity could do the job in a university laboratory!"

He leaned back in his chair and stretched his left leg under his desk. "All right, Sergeant, you can start tracking down the names on your list. You can employ as many detective constables as you need, but somehow I don't think you're going to find anyone named Fiona Smith."

Burnett smiled faintly, made an acknowledgement and then went out.

Nicolson read the *Times* columns again and then sat thinking hard. He was convinced that here was the source of the nerve gas that had been used on the oil rigs. The mass of reports that had flooded in from all over Europe and North America were all insistent that there had been no theft from any of their military bases or research centers. That left the double blunder in England as the only explanation—unless some rogue Iron Curtain or Arab government had deliberately allowed a horror weapon to pass into terrorist hands.

92

Here was Counter-Terror's supreme nightmare, the one that woke them up sweating blood, and he hardly dared to think about it.

Harry Stone spared him. There was a knock on the glass-panelled door and then the burly detective inspector came in with a purposeful tread. His face was bleak as he pushed an envelope and a single sheet of typed paper on to Nicolson's desk.

"I thought you'd want to see this straight away, sir." Stone said. "It was posted yesterday afternoon in Edinburgh and arrived at the offices of the *Daily Mirror* this morning. They've kept a photostat copy which they intend to publish tomorrow. This is the original."

Nicolson read slowly through the brief ultimatum in block capitals.

FROM THE HEADQUARTERS OF THE NEW SCOTTISH LIBERATION ARMY.

WE DEMAND AN END TO THE EXPLOITATION AND POLITICAL DOMINATION OF SCOTLAND. WE DEMAND A SEPARATE CONSTITUTIONAL FREEDOM FOR THE PEOPLE OF SCOTLAND. WE DEMAND A FREE REPUBLIC OF SCOTLAND, INDEPENDENT OF THE UNITED KINGDOM, WITH OUR OWN PARLIAMENT AND COMPLETE CONTROL OF OUR OWN DESTINY AND RESOURCES. WE DEMAND AN END TO THE BLATANT PIRACY OF SCOTLAND'S OFFSHORE OIL RICHES BY AN ENGLISH GOVERNMENT THAT TAKES ALL, POLLUTES AND DESTROYS OUR COUNTRYSIDE AND COASTLINE, AND GIVES BACK NOTHING.

WE SWEAR THAT ENGLAND WILL NEVER PROFIT FROM SCOTLAND'S OIL. WE HAVE ALREADY DESTROYED TWO OF YOUR OFFSHORE OIL RIGS, AND UNLESS OUR DEMANDS ARE MET IN FULL WE SHALL DESTROY MORE.

WE SWEAR THAT SCOTLAND WILL BE FREE.

THE CHIEF OF THE CLANS.

"The Chief of the Clans," Nicolson read the signature aloud and looked up at Stone. "It sounds like someone with historic megalomania!"

"More like someone with a tribal mind," the detective inspector said with weary contempt. "Free Northern Ireland! Free Scotland! Free Cornwall! Free Little-Armpit-in-the-Marsh! It'll be free streets next, and free alleys. Some of them are daft enough to break everything down until we're all barricading ourselves into caves again!"

"But it could be a break for us," Nicolson said. "Now we know that we're looking for an extreme group of Scottish nationalists."

Stone frowned, remembering. "They go back as far as the original Scottish Republican Army that was formed in fifty-two. They were responsible for incidents at the time of the Queen's coronation. Then there was the Army of the Provisional Government of Scotland that was active a couple of years back. They planned a campaign of bombings and assassinations but came to grief when they were caught setting up a bank raid to raise funds. Five of them got prison sentences for conspiracy, but they claimed to have five hundred men operating in clandestine cells modeled on the IRA."

He pushed a hand over his thinning hair, a gesture of exasperation. "Then there was another lot who called themselves the Tartan Army. They blew up a valve house on the oil pipeline to Grangemouth a few months back, and caused another explosion in a pumping station at Perth."

"Do it the easy way," Nicolson advised. "Go and get the files and we'll make a study of all the Mad Jock groups we know."

The *Daily Mirror* published the ultimatum story in sensational black headlines the following morning. A copy was brought back to Strachan Castle by Janis Wallace who had gone into the nearest town with a group

94

from the commune to buy bread and milk and wine. It was late afternoon before Vincenzi read it and brought it grimly to Cobral. The terrorist leader exploded and went fuming in search of Duncan Strachan.

He found the self-styled Chief of the Clans in the ruins of the great hall. The castle was deserted except for Strachan and Bruce Munro who were working together on a Land Rover that needed its plugs and ignition points cleaned and re-set. The other members of the New Scottish Liberation Army were engaged in weapons training under the direction of Hugh Cameron somewhere in the vast sweep of the forest that began beyond the castle walls.

Cobral slammed down the hood of the Land Rover with a crash and slapped the newspaper on top. His voice was vibrant with barely suppressed anger.

"Are you responsible for this?"

Strachan glanced at the headline and then into the black blaze of Cobral's eyes. He squared his broad shoulders and planted his feet more firmly on the grassy earth, a gesture and a stance that suggested he was ready for anything. His hands were on his hips and his black beard bristled over his hardening jaw.

"Ay," he answered bluntly. "I wrote it."

"And I took it into Edinburgh to post it." Munro spoke softly. There were grease smears on his face and in his tangled hair. He was wiry and muscular beneath his dirty hippie denims and as he straightened up there was a large spanner gripped casually in his right hand.

Cobral chose to ignore him, concentrating on Strachan.

"You're a fool," he said savagely. "Don't you realize what you've done?"

"I've told the blasted Sassenachs who we are and what we stand for," Strachan said harshly. "There's no harm in that."

"You've put our whole operation at risk." Cobral left the urge to grip his thick-headed ally by the throat and shake him out of his stupidity. "By making the involvement of your group public knowledge you may have given the English police a lead that will bring them straight here."

"Maybe, but you forget why we're doing this. We're fighting for freedom and independence for Scotland, and the English have to know that. Our aims are not going to be pushed aside by the fancy world ambitions of your precious Terror Incorporated."

"Without my organization you are nothing. Alone your pathetic little army is capable of no more than placing a simple bomb on a pipeline, causing damage that can be repaired in a matter of hours. This operation is something far more vital. Something far too important to be put at risk by a crazy letter to a newspaper."

"Our cause had to be made known. That was my decision."

"Your cause! Do you not yet understand that a local revolution is almost certainly doomed to failure? I have fought in such a revolution when all the circumstances seemed in our favor and still watched our hopes collapse. It is too easy for a government to crush a local revolution. That is why a revolutionary must be born in one country and trained in another to attack a third. Successful revolution can only be worldwide with terror as the supreme weapon."

"My only concern is Scotland," Strachan snapped. "That's what I'm fighting for. And you just remember that you need us much more than we need you. It was my sister who got hold of the formula for the nerve gas. And it's Hugh Cameron and myself who turned the old dungeons here into a laboratory to make the stuff. Every time we handle it we risk our lives, and don't you forget it. You wouldn't be attacking the oil rigs at all without our help!"

"It is not a question of gratitude." Cobral was trembling with impotent rage. "This ultimatum was an unnecessary risk."

"It'll lead the English police nowhere," Munro said carelessly. "I told you, I went all the way to bloody Edinburgh to post it."

Cobral knew that he was wasting his time. He couldn't reverse what had already been done. "The next time, please consult me," he thundered. Then he clawed the newspaper up into his fist and strode away.

Duncan Strachan watched him go, then he looked at Munro and shrugged his shoulders. Munro grinned and they both returned their attention to the ailing Land Rover.

Hamish, the last Earl of Strachan, sat rigid in his wheelchair in the small room in the south wing of the castle. His bony hands were knotted white with tension where they rested on the plaid blanket that covered his useless legs. His jaw was grey with stubble and the lines and wrinkles on his ancient face were etched deeper than ever before.

He had heard the raised voices in the great hall below and every word of the shouted argument had carried clearly through his open window. Now at last he knew what was happening, and why he was virtually a prisoner in his own home.

Again he cursed and cursed his paralyzed limbs. If he could have had life and strength and the power of movement! He began to weep at the thought.

ELEVEN

It was noon when Gloria Kasler drove her Ford Mustang convertible into Hillside, a town of three thousand population and one main street that made a lazy curve around the foot of the hill. She parked in front of the only supermarket, shut off the ignition and climbed out on to the hot sidewalk. She wore red shorts, a white blouse knotted at the waist and sun-glasses. She glanced up and down the empty street and wondered what it would take to wake this town up. An earthquake maybe, or World War Three; nothing less would ever shake Hillside out of its lethargy.

She went into the store—the supermarket label was really a bit too much. Fred Harrison, the skinny old man who ran the place, was sitting behind one of the two cash registers. The other was closed and the two girls he employed were obviously away on their lunch break. Harrison gave her a nod and said good morning. When evening came he would still be saying good morning, Gloria thought sarcastically. Change of any sort took a long time in Hillside.

There were a couple of other women shoppers but no one she knew. Gloria took a wire trolley and pushed it around the shelves, filling it up with all the foodstuffs they needed back at the ranch. At the meat freezer she hesitated. She was getting sick of beefsteak, but the Arabs ate them for breakfast and dinner as though they had never seen meat before. Where they came from they must have starved for the last twenty years.

She was leaning into the freezer when she heard the approaching roar. At first it sounded like a juggernaut truck thundering into the south end of town, but then the noise swelled into the snarling fury of a dozen powerful engines, each trying to outgun the others. She looked up as it reached a deafening crescendo and saw the heavy motorcycles with their wild, black-garbed riders streaking past the windows.

The sound ebbed and then swelled again as the motorcycles turned around and came back. The riders stopped in front of the supermarket, some of them sitting back on their machines and twisting the throttles open with the clutch in, while two rode around in ear-blasting circles. As if the noise of their machines was not enough the riders hooted and yelled at each other like rampaging Indians on the warpath. Except that they were not Indians. The whole gang consisted of tough young Negroes.

Gloria Kasler watched them through the window. She saw two of the young blacks haul their gleaming, psychedelic steel monsters up on to their stands and then come swaggering towards the store. One was a six-foot giant with a black leather jacket unzipped to show an iron cross and a bike chain hung around his neck. He turned to shout back at one of his whooping friends. The name *Ike Death* was printed in silver studs across his massive shoulders. His companion had a frizzy African hairstyle that made him look even taller. He wore a black waistcoat with a skull and crossbones insignia in white stitching, and his bare arms were powerful and muscular.

The two gang leaders pushed into the store. Gloria Kasler moved warily out of sight behind one of the shelves. The other women shoppers moved to join her, one of them clasping her hands over her ears to shut out the roaring of the bikes in the street. Fred Harrison's face had lost some of its normal red color.

"I don't want no trouble," the old man said defensively.

"Hey, Charley!" Ike Death boomed with laughter. "Ole Granpop here says he don't want no trouble!"

"Well, Ah sho am pleased about that!" The black face under the huge black bush of hair grinned rudely as Charley laid on the exaggerated accent. "Ah was just about pissin' mah drawers and shittin' in mah shoes at the thought of ole Granpop here givin' us some trouble." He pushed his face close to Harrison and beamed. "Are yo sho about that, Granpop? Are yo really sho yo don't want no trouble?"

Harrison gulped, his red turkey neck jerking. "Please, boys," he said. "I didn't mean anything."

"Hey, man." Ike Death dropped a huge black paw on Harrison's wincing shoulder. "You ain't got no call to be scared of us. All we want is a dozen cans of beer, and if you move your ass fast enough to get them over here, why, we might even pay you for them."

"Yessir," Charley said. "Go, man! Go, man, go!"

Harrison got up in a hurry. He returned with three four-can packs and put them trembling on the counter. Charley ripped a can out, opened it and began to drink. Ike Death made a pantomime show of searching his pockets.

"Hey, Charley, I ain't got any bread."

"You ain't got any bread!" Charley looked astonished. "I ain't got any bread!"

"It's free," Harrison said quickly. "On the house."

Ike Death bellowed with laughter again. Then he slapped a five dollar bill on top of the cash register.

"We only funnin' you, ole man. Keep the change and have a can yourself."

They went out still laughing and threw beer cans at the rest of their group.

The roar of the motorcycles died as the gang shut

down or switched off to drink beer. Gloria Kasler and the other two women looked at each other dubiously and then continued to fill their shopping baskets. Gloria made the job last but when she eventually wheeled her full trolley back to the cash desk the motorcycle riders were still outside. She could see them standing or sitting astride their machines, talking and laughing out loud.

Harrison counted up and stacked her groceries into a large cardboard box. "Thirty-five dollars and seventy cents," he said at last.

Gloria paid him. Harrison rang up and gave her the change, then he looked over his shoulder.

"I wouldn't go out there just yet, Mrs. Kasler. Those boys have a crazy sense of humor. You're welcome to stay in the store until they leave."

Gloria hesitated, biting her lip. Then she made up her mind. "They look as though they could sit out there and drink beer all afternoon. And the more beer they drink the worse they'll get. I think I'll take a chance and leave now."

Harrison nodded and looked unhappy. Normally he would carry the heavy box of groceries out to the car for her, but after a minute she realized that he wasn't going to move out of the store. She picked up the box and carried it out for herself.

A chorus of hoots and wolf whistles greeted her as she stepped on to the sidewalk. At least two of the gang were girls and their catcalls were the worst.

"Hey, white chick, is your ass the same color as mine?"

"Hey, Charley, why don't you bang that? I'll bet she ain't as hot as I am!"

Gloria tightened her lips and walked quickly, almost running to the car. She had to set the grocery box down on the sidewalk to open the door and then she saw that both nearside tires on the Ford Mustang were flat. She straightened up slowly, feeling panic. She walked round the front of the car and saw that all four wheel rims were down on the road. The tires had been slashed with a knife.

There was a massed roaring as the motorcycles started up. The riders wheeled them in a slow circle around the lone white woman and the immobilized car. Gloria looked up and saw black faces taunting her, their white teeth laughing between thick lips. The noise deafened her as they revved their engines and the smell of petrol and exhaust fumes made her suddenly feel sick. One of the glittering 500cc bikes squeezed between her and the car, its rider's thigh brushing her buttocks and causing her to move quickly forward.

"What's wrong, white chick, you're looking pale?"

"Is there something wrong with your nice new car?"

"Smile at me, honeychile. Why you white babes always so miserable?"

Gloria looked round desperately but there was no help in sight. Right now she could have prayed for Sheriff Dan Parker but there was never a lawman around when one was wanted. The rest of Hillside either had no guts or they were still asleep.

"Them tires don't look much good, baby. Poor quality tires they put on cars these days."

The speaker sat astride his machine and made a show of cleaning his nails with a sharp knife. Gloria knew instinctively that it was the same knife that had cut her tires but she didn't dare accuse him of it. She made a dive back to the store but a motorcycle headed her off. The riders began to wheel their machines around her a little faster, a bright, circling wall of hot, savage steel.

Charley pulled into the center of the circle and stopped beside her. He was grinning and she was both excited and repelled by the black muscles of his arms.

"You ain't goin' nowhere in that car, baby. If you got somewhere to go why don't you let ole Charley give you a ride?"

"Ole Charley one of the best riders there is," one of

the black girls shouted from the back of a bike, and then she howled with laughter.

"Please," Gloria said. "Please let me go."

"You a good-looking chick. With ole Charley you can go anywhere you like." He reached out a fist and caught the knot of her blouse. "Or do anything you like. Anything you'd like to do with ole Charley?"

"Let me go!" Gloria screamed and broke away.

She began to run but immediately there was a snarl of power behind her as Charley opened up his throttle. The other members of the gang widened their circle across the full width of the street, giving Gloria room to run inside with Charley's machine chasing at her heels. There were more howls of laughter and hoots of encouragement. The lifted dust choked Gloria's throat and then she stumbled and fell. Charley wrenched at his raised handlebars to avoid her and his booted foot and the steel barrel of his exhaust swept close past her face.

Gloria screamed again, closed her eyes and rolled away.

When she opened her eyes she could see through a gap in the barrier of motorcycles. A large black Chevrolet sedan had entered town from the north and pulled to a stop. A big man climbed out slowly, another Negro, but this time an adult in a smart blue suit. He had an amiable face that now looked angry.

The big man pushed purposefully into the ring of bikes and the riders suddenly fell silent. A large hand helped Gloria Kasler to her feet and she stared uncertainly.

"Are you hurt, ma'am?" the big man asked.

Gloria was afraid to answer. Charley had heaved his bike on to its stand and wandered back with his hands on his hips.

"She ain't hurt," Charley said. "We was just havin' a little fun. She slipped. That's all."

A pair of dark brown, steady and quietly dangerous

eyes fixed on Charley. "The fun is over," Wayne Johnson said.

Charley smiled at him, a big wide, arrogant smile. Then he spread his hands and shrugged his shoulders. "Okay, Uncle Tom, we ain't lookin' for no trouble."

He turned and walked away towards his bike. He made two very casual steps and then suddenly whipped round. His right hand was coming away from his belt with a weighted blackjack which he swung viciously at Johnson's head. Johnson blocked the swing with his left fist and his right crashed into Charley's jaw. Charley went over backwards and lay spreadeagled in the dust.

There were howls of anger. One youth gunned his engine and roared his powerful motorcycle straight at Johnson from the opposite side of the road. Johnson turned like a bullfighter, catching the handlebars of the machine as it went past. He heaved with a fantastic show of strength and threw both the machine and rider sideways down the street. The rider spilled off. The machine lay bellowing with its back wheel spinning furiously.

"He smashed a bike!"

"Get that big nigger bastard!"

They were really angry now but they were not risking their precious machines. The gang rushed Johnson on foot and Gloria cowered back against her Ford Mustang and watched. She saw Johnson explode into a dazzling display of unarmed combat that was almost too fast for her eye to follow. Three more members of the motorcycle gang went crashing out of the fight and then a bull voice roared:

"Get outa the goddamned way! *Let me have him!*"

The struggling mob around Johnson broke away and left him to stand alone. Ike Death faced him with an animal snarl and the heavy cycle chain swinging in his massive hand. Johnson waited and let him come with a rush. The chain whirled like a black steel snake, striking for Johnson's neck. Johnson ducked beneath it and smashed his fist into Ike Death's huge belly. His knee slammed up into Ike Death's groin. Ike Death let out a monstrous groan and then an uppercut finished him. He fell like a collapsing mountain.

Johnson stepped back again and waited, but it was over. Those who had breath left helped those who hadn't and the subdued gang crawled on to their machines and drove slowly away. When the street was empty and the dust had settled Johnson pulled out a handkerchief and dabbed blood from his cut mouth. Then he walked over and helped Gloria Kasler to her feet.

"I sure am sorry about that, ma'am." He spoke apologetically as though it was all his own fault. "It embarrasses me to see black kids jostling a white woman like that. I hope it don't make you think bad of all black men."

"No." Gloria didn't want to meet his eyes as she dusted herself down. She was bruised and shaken and she didn't know what to say. She added lamely, "Thank you for your help."

"It was my pleasure. I'm glad I happened by." Johnson looked down at the flat tires of the Mustang. "Did those punk kids do that?"

"I guess so."

Johnson walked round the car and came back frowning. "They cut them all bad. You're going to need four new tires. I have a tow rope, so if you want I can pull you back to that gas station that's up the road a way."

Gloria bit her lip. She didn't see any alternative and so she accepted the offer. Johnson backed his Chevrolet in front of the Mustang and then produced a wire-cored rope to link the two cars together. He loaded the box of groceries into the Mustang and then started his own car. Gloria steered the Mustang and he pulled her half a mile to the gas station and garage that was on the south edge of town. While he retrieved the rope she got out and talked with the gas pump attendant and two me-

106

chanics. Soon she was looking frustrated and angry again.

"What's the problem?" Johnson asked.

"They haven't got enough tires in stock," Gloria said in exasperation.

"We've only got two of this particular size," one of the mechanics explained. "We can't get the others until tomorrow."

Johnson sighed. "How far do you have to go?"

"My husband has a small ranch and an airfield about eight miles out of town," Gloria told him.

"Does your husband have another vehicle?"

"He's got a beat-up old station wagon."

"Okay. How about me taking you home now. You can come back with your husband in the station wagon to pick up the Mustang."

Gloria hesitated. "I don't want to bother you."

"It's no bother." He gave her an amiable smile. "They were my color skin who got you into this mess, and I ain't proud of them. It's the least I can do."

Fifteen minutes later the black Chevrolet pulled up in front of the Kasler ranch house. Johnson and Gloria got out and moved to the back of the car. Johnson opened up the trunk and Gloria leaned inside for the big cardboard box filled with groceries. Johnson stopped her.

"That thing is heavy. Let me carry it for you."

"It's okay." Gloria tried to stall. She had recovered her wits now and all that she wanted was to get rid of this big black man. She knew that Frank and the others must be watching and wondering what the hell was going on. "You've done enough," she said. "I'm grateful."

She tried to lift the box but Johnson took it out of her hands.

"I insist, you just lead the way."

Gloria felt panic again, but this time she couldn't let it show. She didn't want to be rude and she knew she couldn't afford to be rude, that might make him suspect that something was wrong. She held back with her mind in an undecided whirl but then Johnson took the decision away from her by heading for the ranch house with the box in his arms.

She caught him up, got ahead and hesitated again by the door. Johnson waited, smiling at her over the cereal boxes, the sliced bread and the milk bottles that were sticking up out of the box. She couldn't just let him stand there. She smiled back at him faintly and hoped to Christ that the Arab jokers had enough sense to stay out of sight. Reluctantly she opened the door.

"You can put it on the table," she said. She hoped her voice sounded normal.

Johnson did as he was asked. The room was big and comfortable, serving as a lounge and a dining room. There were straight-backed chairs round the table and a couple of big leather armchairs over by the open fireplace. There was an open plan staircase to his left, with one closed door under it. Two more closed doors led off to his right.

Frank Kasler stood in the center of the room, his hands dangling awkwardly at his sides. It might have been the sad droop of his moustaches but Johnson thought that his creased face looked unhappy. Johnson beamed cheerfully. Kasler's face stayed the same.

"This is Frank, my husband," Gloria said quickly. "Frank, this is Mister—?"

"Johnson," Johnson said. "But you can call me Wayne. My mother, God bless her, was a fan of the Big Duke. Would you believe she saw *Stagecoach* twenty-seven times! When I came along I just had to be called Wayne." He beamed at them some more.

"Hello," Kasler said, but the word was half strangled somewhere inside his throat.

"I had some trouble in town," Gloria hurried to explain. "A bunch of kids cut up the tires on the Mustang. Mister Johnson was good enough to bring me home."

108

Kasler continued to stare for several seconds before he realized that she had spoken. Then he struggled to offer his thanks.

"They were black kids," Johnson said. "When a man sees his own color kids doing wrong, it seems like he's obliged to try and put it right. I'm really sorry Mrs. Kasler got roughed up."

"Yeah," Kasler said vaguely. He had a cue to show some concern for his wife but obviously there was a lot more on his mind.

There was an uncomfortable silence.

"Nice place you have here," Johnson offered.

"Yeah," Kasler said again.

Johnson waited like a man who expected to be offered a cup of coffee. Kasler wet his lips and suddenly fumbled for his wallet in his hip pocket.

"It must have cost you a few dollars gas money to get out here?"

"Please don't," Johnson raised his hands. "I'd be offended."

Kasler put the wallet back. There was more silence.

"I'd better be going," Johnson said at last.

Kasler looked relieved. Gloria looked relieved and embarrassed. They both offered their thanks again.

Johnson turned to go. He had already noticed that three of the five chairs around the dining table looked as though they had been rescued from the lumber room to seat unexpected guests. Also the grocery box had been far too heavy to suit the needs of just two people. Then there were Kasler's reactions, and the prickly feeling at the back of his own neck which told him that the three of them were not alone here. It all added up to the fact that Dan Parker's suspicions had been right.

Johnson had no more doubts, but he still wanted to draw the hidden listeners into the open. He wanted a look at their faces.

The tense, explosive atmosphere suggested a way. Johnson had the feeling that if so much as a pin dropped here then the whole bunch of them would over-react like scalded cats. He looked for an alternative to a pin and saw a tall vase of cut flowers on a small table by the door.

Deliberately clumsy, he banged his heel against the table leg as he backed up to the door saying goodbye. The tall vase wobbled, overbalanced and fell with a sudden crash to the floor.

It was like a gunshot and forced an immediate response that was far more positive and violent than he had calculated. The door beneath the stairs burst open and two dark-faced men sprang like wildcats into the room.

Rashid dropped into a crouch with his machine pistol raised and sighted on Johnson's chest. Jemal moved past him with a black Luger automatic in his hand.

TWELVE

The special flight from Caracas to Houston landed three hours later. A gangway was rushed into position as the giant Douglas DC-8 airliner rolled to a stop, and a waiting police car cruised up to the foot of the gangway. Steve Regan hurried out of the plane and into the car. Immediately it made a fast half circle turn and sped back to the airport exit with its light flashing and the siren howling. It was a reverse performance of Regan's hectic arrival three days before and he leaned back wearily in the passenger seat. By now he was beginning to feel like a human ping pong ball being battered from country to country.

Detective Lieutenant Roy Hanson was at the wheel. He welcomed his chief and Regan made acknowledgement but it was all very brief.

"What's the excitement?" Regan demanded. "The details were a bit vague in Caracas. All I really know is that Wayne wanted me back in one hell of a hurry."

Hanson told him, explaining rapidly.

"Agent Johnson wanted me here to sift reports and handle the paperwork build-up on the spot," Hanson finished. "He also wanted a specialized action team so I flew down from New York with Clinton and North. They're waiting at Hillside. That's where we're going."

Regan nodded approval. FBI agents Clinton and North were on permanent transfer to Counter-Terror. They worked as a hit team, either as a pair or as the

111

dual spearhead of a commando task force. Either way they were the best in the business.

It was dusk when they arrived at Hillside and they found the commandeered sheriff's office ready for war. There were police vehicles, patrol cars and even a couple of armored cars lining the street outside. The area swarmed with uniformed police officers, plainclothes FBI men, sheriff's deputies, the motorcycle gang and a dozen tall, hard-faced men who looked as though they might have been a Green Berets team airlifted straight out of the jungles of Vietnam. They wore black uniforms, soft guerrilla hats, black ceramic body armor, and a bristling array of automatic weapons that ranged from light machine guns to gas guns.

"The Houston SWAT Squad," Hanson explained as they got out of the car. SWAT stood for Special Weapons And Tactics. "Those guys are real combat-hungry. There's a couple of helicopters standing by to fly them in with all guns blazing if we need them."

"Like hell," Regan said. "I want my Deputy Section Head back in one piece!"

They went into the crowded office. The FBI Field Director for the State of Texas Regan already knew. They had cooperated in Galveston. Agents Clinton and North were also familiar. They sat side by side, two well groomed and very presentable young men in dark, neatly cut suits. They looked the type of smart, polite young men whom any respectable banker's daughter would be only too happy to take home to daddy. Except that daughter and daddy would both have a heart attack if they ever saw these two engaged in their normal line of business. They were ex-gangbusters supreme, now dedicated to smashing terrorists.

The other men were strangers but Hanson swiftly introduced them. Sheriff Jameson. Deputy Sheriff Parker. And FBI Agents Mallory and Green, both from the Houston Field Office.

112

Agent Green was Ike Death. Agent Mallory was Charley.

They talked for ten minutes while Regan studied maps of the area and a large sketch plan of the Kasler ranch and airfield. The latter had been drawn by Dan Parker whose knowledge of that particular section of the local terrain was even better than the sheriff's.

"You say there's a range of low hills behind the ranch house." Regan looked at Parker. "Now that it's dark, just how close do you think we could get before they nail us down?"

Parker looked through the window. "No stars and no moon," he observed. "Ordinarily, I'd reckon I could get right up to the back door. But how close you're gonna get that small army outside is another question."

"Forget them," Regan said bluntly. "We're not shooting a TV film, and if I wanted the place razed to the ground I could call up the air force, or a tank with a flamethrower. I'm talking about a simple three-man hit. Just myself, Agent Clinton, and Agent North."

Parker looked at the two poker faces and smiled slowly. "For city boys they look as though they might tread soft. I reckon maybe I can get you close enough."

"Good." Regan had an instinctive confidence in the slow-drawling deputy sheriff. He turned to agents Mallory and Green. "But we're still going to need a diversion of some kind. How about your team giving another performance of *The Wild Ones*?"

The two Negros exchanged grins.

"As long as Wayne Johnson don't have to hit me again," Mallory said, and rubbed ruefully at his bruised jaw.

At that moment Johnson was in no position to hit anyone. He was roped to one of the straight-backed chairs at the Kasler ranch house with his wrists pulled tight together behind his back. Rashid sat on the pine-board table in front of him with the machine pistol supported on his thigh and the muzzle aimed at Johnson's head. Sharaf had returned and viciously tonguelashed his two lieutenants for their initial hasty move, but the damage had been done. Since then they had all argued for four hours without being able to decide what to do with him.

Throughout Johnson had acted bewildered and maintained that he wasn't a police officer of any kind. He was, he kept repeating, just a guy who had seen a woman in trouble and helped her out. He didn't know what this was all about.

"That no longer matters." Sharaf had finally shut him up savagely. "Thanks to these fools I cannot let you go. Even if you are innocent, you now know that my friends and I are here. I cannot allow you to depart."

"It's not my fault," Gloria snapped. He had included her in the general circle of fools and she was resentful. "If your two trigger-happy gorillas hadn't jumped him just because he knocked a vase over he would have been miles away by now. He was on his way out and he would have known nothing!"

Sharaf towered over her, his dark face black with fury. "You brought him here! You are as stupid as they are."

Gloria bit her lip and backed away. Her face was pale and her heart was suddenly hammering. She had not been afraid of them before, not like Frank who was afraid of what they were doing, but she was afraid now. For the first time she realized how utterly merciless Sharaf could be. The lives of his friends would be cheap, the lives of his enemies less than nothing.

Kasler had opened a bottle of bourbon with shaking hands. He was now on his fifth drink and they had all been hefty shots. He was too far gone to take notice of his wife's or Sharaf's face. He just cradled his glass in both hands and mumbled, "What are we gonna do? Just what the hell are we gonna do?"

114

"You have to do nothing," Sharaf told him with contempt. "Rashid and Jamal will take this man back into the hills and bury him."

Kasler almost became sober. He stared up into the eagle eyes.

"That's murder! They could fry me for that! The electric chair, don't you know what that means?"

"You do not have to do it."

"I don't want any part of it! Jesus Christ, they could pull me in as an accessory. I don't want no murder rap!"

"The decision is not yours," Sharaf said with contempt.

Kasler took refuge in his drink. Gloria stared horrified. Rashid and Jemal registered nothing.

"The man could be right," Johnson said hopefully. "I don't know why you people should want to kill me, but if you do it's murder. I was only passing through but there's people in town who saw me drive up here with Mrs. Kasler. For instance, the mechanics at the gas station where we left the Mustang."

"You were only passing through." Jemal smiled coldly as he repeated the words. "You admit that you are a stranger here. No one will care if you do not return."

"My wife will care if I don't get back to Houston some time tonight. Then the law will start looking for me. Eventually they must find out that I came here."

"But that will all take time." Sharaf looked at his two friends. "After this we must make the next flight tomorrow. We must finish our task here quickly and leave."

"Perhaps we can keep him here as a prisoner until you're gone," Gloria suggested doubtfully. She still wasn't sure whether she owed Johnson a favor.

Sharaf turned slowly to stare at her and that was reprimand enough. Gloria bit her lip and turned away trembling. Sharaf scowled at the back of her neck but then decided to ignore her. When he resumed the discussion with Rashid and Jemal all the rest of their talk was in Arabic.

It was half an hour later when they decided that it was dark enough to move. Jemal went out of the room and when he returned he was carrying a spade. The Kaslers looked at it as though hypnotized but maintained their helpless silence. Rashid slid off the table and aimed his machine pistol very carefully while Sharaf used a sharp knife to cut Johnson free from the chair. Johnson's wrists were still tied behind his back and he continued to sit.

"Stand up," Sharaf ordered after he had stepped back.

Johnson stood up slowly.

Kasler broke his eyes away from the spade in Jemal's hand and poured himself another bourbon. Some of it missed the glass and spilled over his shaking wrist.

Gloria swallowed hard on nothing.

"You can walk out through the back," Sharaf told Johnson. "Rashid and Jemal will follow."

"And if I don't?" Johnson had stopped pretending now and he stared back at the Arab.

Sharaf shrugged. "If you make it easy, we can make it painless."

Johnson hesitated, feeling his balance and reasoning. Here in the lighted room he had no chance. Outside in the dark, especially if Sharaf stayed back to watch the Kaslers, then maybe one of the others would put a foot wrong. He only needed Rashid to stumble once.

"Okay," he said slowly. "But I still don't understand why."

He looked towards Gloria Kasler but she wouldn't meet his eyes. Finally he shrugged his broad shoulders and turned away. It was then that they heard the beginning of the high-powered drone from the night outside. Johnson stopped. The three Arabs exchanged uncertain

116

glances and Sharaf moved fast to the window. The drone gathered in volume to a mechanical roar. Johnson turned his head and saw the white headlight beams lancing through the darkness as the motorcycles swept up the dirt track to the ranch house.

Jemal dropped his spade and pulled out his automatic. Sharaf produced another.

The bellowing motorcycles reached the front of the ranch house in a shower of gravel from skidding tires and a thunder of revving engines. They formed a half circle facing the door and the window where Sharaf watched and the noise abated by a few barely noticeable decibels as two of the machines were switched off. The riders were howling and yelling in an unintelligible animal chorus. Two figures moved forward into the blazing circle of headlights, throwing monstrous shadows in all directions.

Ike Death and Charley.

The two gang leaders were staggering and they looked drunk. Charley had a whisky bottle tilted to his mouth and he leaned on Ike Death's shoulder for support. Ike Death had a glazed look in his eyes and he planted his feet as though he was unsure of his balance.

"Bring out that big buck nigger!" Ike Death roared. "This time we're gonna fix him real good!"

"Yeah!" Charley shouted in a slurred voice. "We saw him drive up here. Send him out and we gonna rip his balls off. He ain't gonna get the better of us twice!"

Ike Death waved his bike chain in a massive fist. Charley broke away from him and smashed his empty bottle on the handle bars of the nearest machine and brandished the jagged edges toward the ranch house.

"Bring him out," they bawled together. "Or we gonna come in there and get him!"

Inside the ranch house Gloria Kasler had gone white. "It's the same bunch," she said hoarsely. "They must have got liquored up somewhere."

Nobody answered her. The three Arabs stared at each other uncertainly. They had the firepower to withstand a siege but it was the last thing they wanted.

"Perhaps we should send him out." Frank Kasler suddenly saw it as the easy way out of his own dilemma. "Perhaps those guys out there will kill him. That way he's dead and we don't get the blame."

"No." There was a sheen of sweat around Sharaf's dark eyes but he was still not convinced. "Perhaps they are his friends. Or perhaps they will not quite kill him but leave him alive somewhere."

Outside Ike Death lurched over to Johnson's black Chevrolet sedan. He swung his bike chain and caved in the nearside headlight in a crash of breaking glass.

"We know he's still in there," he yelled at the ranch house. "This is his car!" He swung the chain again at the second headlight. The third swing shattered the windshield and then he began slashing wildly at the car body.

The other riders and Charley howled their approval and added to the uproar.

Fear sobered Frank Kasler sufficiently to find himself a shotgun. Sharaf and his two friends began to argue in frantic Arabic. Johnson sat down in his chair again, pretending to look scared, and patiently waited.

Dan Parker halted in a shallow, stone-littered gully, crouching silently behind a low outcrop of rock. Steve Regan knelt beside him. In the darkness they had barely visible shadows. The shadows were Clinton and North.

All three of the Counter-Terror men wore black. They had black sweaters, black slacks and black, rubber-soled shoes. They all had black hair and they all carried Colt .45 automatics. The Colt was manstopper enough for the job and they didn't want to be weighed down by a rattling armory.

They were surrounded by black hills but ahead there

118

was a gap through which they could see one wing of the ranch house and the white glare of lights beyond. So far they had made less noise than a single stalking coyote, but under cover of the racket Green and Mallory were making Regan reflected that they could have got this close unnoticed in a truck.

Parker pointed through the gap. "You just follow this gully straight down," he said softly. "That'll lead you right up to Frank's back door. The door lets you into the kitchen. It's probably locked but there's a side window. On a warm night like this it could be open. Left side of the house there's a big window that looks into the main living and dining area. Right hand side two windows look into the bedrooms."

Parker paused and let his hand rest on his holstered revolver. "I wouldn't mind coming with you if you need another gun."

Regan smiled. "I'm sorry, Sheriff, but these two boys don't even want me along! Clinton here knows exactly what North is going to do, how he's going to think and which way he's liable to jump. And North knows exactly the same about Clinton. They figure that anyone else is only liable to get in the way. I'm only going because I'm their boss and it's my buddy who is trapped in there. I'm pulling rank."

Clinton and North permitted themselves two faint and slightly clinical smiles. Parker knew when he was not wanted and moved his shoulders in a shrug.

"I'll stay here and cover in case any of them get past you," he said. His tone didn't hold any hope that he would really be needed.

Inside the ranch house there was the smell of fear. Frank Kasler stood by the window with the shotgun and the bourbon poured out of him in sweat. He wanted to throw Johnson out to the mob but the three Arabs were still undecided. Sharaf stood on the opposite side of the window and argued with his friends. Rashid was poised by the door while Jemal stood well back to cover Johnson with his automatic.

Rashid wanted to step outside with his machine pistol and fire a burst over the heads of the rioting Negroes to drive them away. Sharaf didn't want to reveal their presence here and also he was afraid that if this was a police trap then his hotblooded companion would be cut down by a sniper's rifle. Sharaf still wasn't sure that what was happening could be taken at face value and the uncertainty and the weight of his responsibilities as group commander were making him sweat almost as much as Kasler.

Outside Ike Death and Charley were still venting their spite on the car. They led the rest of the gang in a violent mass movement to rock the big Chevrolet up and down until they finally succeeded in hurling it over. As the car rolled and crashed heavily on to its roof there was another wild burst of cheering.

The three Arabs moved closer to the window to stare out.

"Now we want the big buck!" Charley yelled. "We finished playin' games now. We all comin' in to get that big nigger bastard!"

Ike Death and Charley started to move towards the ranch house. The rest of the leather-jacketed young Negroes followed in a close packed mob.

Rashid moved to yank open the front door without Sharaf's orders. He had had enough and it was time to start shooting.

Then the long window that ran along the left hand side of the room exploded into breaking glass as a fist-sized rock was hurled through it.

Sharaf spun with his automatic raised to meet the new threat. His reactions were fast even though he had been taken by surprise.

The grim face of Steve Regan showed for a split second, framed in the jagged glass spears of the broken window. Regan fired once and the bullet from the big Colt smashed Sharaf's collar bone.

Rashid wheeled with the machine pistol and ripped a burst through the window. Regan had already ducked back.

In the same split second the door at the back of the room was booted open. Clinton came through the opening in a shallow dive that had all the speed and ferocity of a black killer shark making its final lunge. He skidded to the left on his chest and elbows, made one neat roll to avoid a bullet from Jemal's automatic that thudded into the floorboards behind him, and then shot Rashid just under the left shoulder blade as he tried to turn back from his futile demolition of the final glass shreds hanging in the window frame.

Jemal moved his automatic to find Clinton again but one shot was all that he was allowed. North stepped calmly through the open doorway. It was his foot that had kicked it wide to make way for Clinton's racing dive, and now he had all the time he would ever need for precision shooting. The big Colt in his hand roared twice. The first bullet hit Jemal dead center in the heart. The second bullet hit Rashid dead center in the heart.

Kasler still stood trembling with the shotgun in his hands.

"Drop it!" Regan snapped from the window behind him.

Kasler obeyed. He knew that he hadn't got the guts to use it and he was almost sick with relief.

Wayne Johnson slowly turned his head and smiled at Regan.

"Is it safe for a man to move now?" he asked.

THIRTEEN

In the North Sea a force ten gale was blowing. The sixty-mile-per-hour winds, whipped up in the bitter, freezing waters of the Arctic, drove the mountainous black waves southwest through the vast black curtains of ice-cold rain. The waves smashed at the lonely oil rigs north of the Shetlands, pounding and shaking the swaying platforms in a brief, blind rage before surging on. They thundered down into the firths of Dornoch and Moray, dinosaurs of salt water thrashing their heads and tails and roaring through foam-flecked jaws. They broke upon the coastlines of Scotland, savaging the stark black cliffs of Caithness, and falling in fury upon jagged rocks below Strachan Castle. Whips of rain, wielded by the mighty hands of the winds, lashed at the ruined walls as though this night they were determined to finish the crumbling destruction of the centuries.

Hamish Strachan sat in his wheelchair in the room that had become his prison and listened to the howling of the elements as they assaulted his ancestral home. His lined face was tense but he was not afraid of the storm. He had lived here all his life and he knew that the castle could take all this punishment and more. He was strained because tonight he had decided to make an effort to leave, if God was willing and the strength of his arms did not fail him.

An hour before Fiona had brought him his supper, a

tray of hot soup, buttered toast and tea. She had kissed him dutifully as always, her lips briefly brushing his temple, but she had not stopped to talk. The Earl knew that she would not return for the tray until morning and so the food and drink stood cold and untouched on the table.

It was midnight and he hoped that the storm had driven the hippie rabble of the NSLA into their sleeping bags.

He propelled his wheelchair to the door and opened it. The door was not kept locked because Duncan and his friends were confident that he could not maneuver the wheelchair down the steep, stone steps to the level of the great hall. The old man sat still for a moment and then he pulled at the plaid blanket that was tucked around his crippled legs. As though it was the blanket and not his own body that failed him he threw it angrily away.

He did not pause now for there had been plenty of time to sit and ponder. He had tired of all that. He let his shoulders slump forward and reached down between his knees. With his fingertips he could just reach the footboard of the chair between his feet. He pulled at the footboard but it was more difficult than he had thought that it would be. He cursed and tried again. This time he succeeded more abruptly than he had expected. He pitched head first out of the chair as he over-balanced and landed heavily on his right shoulder.

He lay there for a moment with his right hand and arm trapped beneath him. The lower half of his body was still a dead weight with no feeling over which he had no control. Finally he managed to push himself over with his left hand and get his right hand free. He twisted his shoulders to bring himself back on to his stomach again, another struggling and painful effort, and then lay panting to recover his strength.

After a few minutes he began to crawl forward, working with his arms and shoulders and dragging the useless trunk and lower limbs inch by inch through the doorway. It was a long haul across the landing, even those muscles that were alive were more feeble than he had realized, but at last he hooked his hands over the top step. He had a good grip to heave his chin up level with his hands and he stared down at the steep black chasm of the stairwell. The force of gravity would help him now, probably fast enough to break his neck if he was not careful, but that was a risk he was prepared to take.

He reached down for a lower step and again he dragged his paralyzed body forward. He started to slide face-first and there was a moment of panic before his dead hips slithered sideways and slumped against the wall. The steps were a succession of frozen tombstones lapping at his face and his heart hammered wildly.

He needed his hands and arms as brakes as much as tools of motion as he slowly continued his agonizing descent into pitch darkness.

Beneath the flapping, rain-battered canvas of the tent in the roofless great hall the majority of the NSLA had crept into their sleeping bags for warmth, but none of them were asleep. In the darker recesses, away from the single electric light bulb suspended on the tent pole that was run out on an extension cable from the castle, the sleeping bags contained couples where varying degrees of kissing and groping were in progress. The others had split up into two groups. Under the light Duncan Strachan sat with his back to the pole and played cards with Munro and two of the girls. The others were simply drinking and talking.

Janis Wallace was with the larger group. She lay in her sleeping bag with her shoulders propped against her rucksack and there was a bottle of wine in her hand. She was drunk and she was bored and she was sour with the whole bloody scene. All they ever did was talk about what they were going to do. Talk, talk, talk and

125

bloody talk, but they never actually *did* anything. She was beginning to hate everybody.

"Where's that bitch Fiona?" she said suddenly, breaking up the conversation and voicing the jealousy that swirled in dark, bitter undercurrents beneath all her surface frustrations and boredom.

Hugh Cameron lay beside her. He rolled over in his sleeping bag to answer, shifting his weight from his left elbow to his right.

"At this minute I'd say that she's up in her room with the Cobra, probably showing him some good old-fashioned Scottish hospitality."

"With her legs wide open," Janis said crudely. "She's so ugly and skinny it's the only part of her he'd want to look at."

"And since when have you had anything against sex?" Cameron laughed at her through his bush of red beard.

"I just don't see what's so special about Fiona-bloody-Strachan!"

Duncan glanced up briefly at the mention of his sister's name. However, he had a good poker hand and he was on a winning streak. He returned his attention almost immediately to the cards.

"Some of us are beginning to wonder what's so special about Luis-bloody-Cobral," one of the drinking circle countered.

"At least he's got balls," Janis said. "He knows how to screw."

"Is that what you're missing, lass?" Cameron rolled closer, grinning and reaching out one hand to squeeze at her breast. "If you were to ask me nicely now, I just might consider giving you another go myself."

"You're a waste of time." Janis pushed his hand away and tilted the wine bottle to her lips. After a long swallow she looked at him again with another mouthful of scorn. "I've tried all the men here and there's not one of you worth writing home about. You're like single-

126

barrelled shotguns—one bang and you're all finished."

There was a burst of laughter, mostly from the girls, and Cameron tried to throw it back at them.

"Some lasses are uninspiring," he taunted. "With you it's like a swim in an ice-cold loch on a frosty winter's morning—one quick dip is enough!"

The second burst of laughter was mostly male, but the girls in the group were smiling and there were a few chuckles. They were all in a reasonably good humor. Only Janis was feeling vile.

"I'm sick of all this," she complained. "I'm sick of lying around and doing nothing. I'm sick of this rotten castle. I'm sick of living in a stinking tent in a bloody ruin." She tipped back more wine but another grievance had come to the surface and she expanded it. "Why do we have to live in this bloody tent anyway in this bloody lousy weather! Cobral has got his own room. And those two dago friends of his have got their own room! Why the hell shouldn't some of us have those rooms for a change?"

"They're guests, that's why they've got the only habitable rooms." Cameron refused to be drawn into an argument about it and a malicious gleam had come into his eyes. "But now that you're talking about our dago friends, there's a man there to cure your sickness. Vincenzi is in the stables tinkering about with his helicopter, so why don't you sneak up and try Orlando for a new sexual thrill?"

"Orlando the fairy! What would I do with him?"

"Use your imagination, lass."

"At least it might be something different—"

"Something to cure your boredom."

There were ripples of laughter among the challenging circle of voices, almost enough to blot out the rattle of the rain on the ballooning canvas overhead. Janis stared at them, hating them, and suddenly feeling her head swim under the effects of the wine.

"I'll tell you something, lass." Cameron pulled at her

arm. "I dare stake a bottle of wine that you couldn't even get a hard on the man."

"I'll bet another bottle!"

"And I'll bet a third. Three bottles, Janis, and all you have to do is to get him to stand up."

"Go on, Janis—" one of the girls urged. "They deserve to lose their money."

Janis was tempted. The bottle in her hand was empty and she wanted more. She wanted to prove them wrong and suddenly her mood was shifting. It might be worth the effort just for the hell of it. The queer might surprise her. She had never tried a queer before and it might be good for a laugh. To end this bloody boredom any kind of a laugh would be worth having, as long as the laugh was on somebody else.

"You think I couldn't do it?"

"Prove it if you can."

"Right," she decided. "I bloody well will. But if I get a hard on him you'll have to take my word for it."

"Agreed," Cameron said.

Janis unzipped her sleeping bag and got to her feet. She wore a sweater and jeans and swayed unsteadily as she looked round for a coat. One of the men threw her a windcheater and she pulled it over her head and shoulders as she lunged through the door flap of the tent. Howls of hilarity followed her out into the pouring darkness.

Hamish Strachan had reached the foot of the staircase. He was bruised and battered and every muscle in his shoulders and arms ached abominably. He had fallen heavily down the last few steps and needed time to recover his breath.

When he was ready he stretched his arms forward over the cold flagstones of the short corridor that led to an arched doorway and out into the great hall. He found a join in the flagstones and dug his bleeding fingers into the crack. Slowly he pulled himself forward.

Each crack and each flagstone represented a major triumph in his interminable, gruelling crawl to the door. How he would open it when he got there he didn't even know. He could only fight one battle at a time. It was pitch black and he fought blind. There was no sound inside the castle and he fought in silence, biting down the urge to cry out when his fingernails splintered and broke. His fingertips were raw and weakness, old age and dead limbs were terrible weights that threatened to crush his spirit into despair.

He was almost within reach of the heavy wooden door when it crashed inwards. His outstretched hand was swept to one side and crushed against the wall and a sharp groan of pain was ripped through his lips. Mercifully it was lost in the roar of the storm and the gusts of rain that squalled in from the night with the stumbling figure of Janis Wallace.

She clawed off the windcheater jacket and threw it down. "Bloody hyenas!" She shouted back at the catcalls of laughter that were still audible above the noise of the elements.

The old man froze to the floor. The wet windcheater had hit him in the face and he was certain that at any second he would be discovered. Then the girl moved past him, feeling her way along the opposite wall in the darkness. Her foot kicked at his shoulder but she noticed nothing.

Hamish Strachan realized from the slur in her voice that she was too drunk to find the light switch.

Behind her Janis had left the doorway into the storm wide open.

Orlando Savas was reading by the light of his bedside lamp. The book was a Spanish translation of James Bond but he wasn't really interested. Sex and violence on the printed page were no substitute for the real thing. He was awake because it seemed pointless to sleep until

Vincenzi returned. He was a light sleeper and easily disturbed.

He knew that Arturo was embarrassed by the fact that they had to share a room together, which was why he was absent as much as possible, but Savas was not offended. He had come to terms with his own status and with other people's responses and, besides, he had no designs on Arturo Vincenzi. Cobral was his great, unfulfilled homosexual love, and to that he was faithful. He thought of Cobral now, and of Fiona Strachan, guessing that they were together, and the ache and the anger pulsed through him. It was a feeling that made him want to kill, to take his beloved submachine gun and shatter flesh and blood with a hail of bullets. Usually he killed on Cobral's orders, to please Cobral, but he could have killed Fiona Strachan to please himself.

He heard the door open and looked up. He expected Vincenzi but instead it was one of the girl hippies. It was the white-faced one with the blonde hair and the thin breasts. He remembered that her name was Janis. She was dripping rain-water on to the carpet and she gave him a wine-sodden smile.

Savas was bewildered by her presence. He felt a surge of strange emotion that might have been fear.

"What do you want?" he asked blankly.

"Warmth and comfort," Janis said. She moved towards him, staggering slightly. Her eyes were bright and her mouth still shaped its loose smile. "You've got a nice, soft bed, and all I've got is a freezing sleeping bag in a wet tent. So—I've come to join you."

"This is my room!" Savas snapped angrily. "Please get out!"

Janis laughed at him. She crossed her hands over her hips, pulled at the edge of her sweater and hauled it off over her head. She wore no bra and Savas stared horrified at her small bare breasts as they so swiftly appeared. He thought that her bare flesh was the dirty, grey-white color of a slit-open fish, and almost as repulsive.

"These clothes are wet," Janis told him. "I'm going to take them off and get into bed with you."

"Señorita—"

Savas choked back what he was about to say as she sat down on the edge of the bed and caressed his arm.

"What lovely blue pyjamas," Janis giggled. "Somehow I just knew you'd wear blue pyjamas. I even expected little pink flowers on them."

Savas squirmed away from her touch, escaping from the bed on the far side. Janis laughed at the speed of his movements. She decided that it was fun seducing a queer. She unzipped her wet jeans and struggled to kick them free of her legs. She rolled on to her back on the bed to give the final kick. Savas watched her from the doorway. His emotions were churning wildly inside and the heat was building up in his brain.

"Come on," Janis challenged him with open arms. "Why don't you give it a try? Just once, you might even get to like it."

"Get out," Savas begged.

Janis stared at him for a minute and then pushed herself up from the bed. She had only her panties left but she thought that if she took those off too soon he would run away in terror. He certainly looked terrified. She moved towards him, enjoying herself. She felt like a powerful cat stalking a shivering mouse.

"Come on, Orlando," she crooned. "If you can just get a hard on it's worth three bottles of wine."

Savas realized that she was drunk. Disgust filled him but at the same time her words struck a raw nerve. He knew that he was incapable of being aroused by any woman, but he was capable of being cruelly humiliated. Something black and monstrous was growing out of his tortured feelings, and reason was being swamped by the red anger haze before his eyes.

Janis reached for him with both hands, plucking at

131

the cord that held his pyjama trousers and groping for his sex.

"Even you must have *some* balls," she insisted.

Fury exploded within Savas, an overpowering hurricane of rage that dwarfed the wild storm still howling through the ruined ramparts of Strachan Castle. He smashed her away with the heel of his hand and blood suddenly gushed from her nose. Panic and pain flooded her eyes with tears and she began to scream at the sight of his contorted face. She backed away, reeling clumsily in her drunken stupor, and Savas followed her. All he wanted was to get this filth out of his room and he grabbed at her hair with both hands. He heaved with all his strength and threw her bodily through the open doorway.

Janis hit the doorpost with her shoulder, spun round full circle on the landing beyond, and then pitched head first down the black stairwell. She was still screaming when her head crashed on to one of the stone steps half way down. The rest of her fall was marked only by the bumping of her tumbling body.

Duncan Strachan heard faintly the storm-muffled screams from within the castle. He looked up from his cards and listened but all that remained was the shriek of wind and rain.

"That was Janis," Hugh Cameron said with conviction.

Strachan saw his red-bearded lieutenant struggling out of his sleeping bag and reaching for an automatic. That was enough and Strachan dropped his cards and pulled his own automatic from the stolen army holster at his hip. The black rain soaked him as he emerged from the tent but he led the way into the castle at a run. Cameron and Bruce Munro were at his heels.

Savas had descended the stairs and switched on a light in the corridor. Janis lay sprawled at his feet with a pool of blood leaking through her blonde hair and widening over the hard flagstones.

Savas had more blood spots staining his neat blue pajamas.

"The bastard's murdered the lass," Cameron said savagely.

"It was an accident," Savas said hoarsely. He guessed that they had all been drinking and began to back warily up the stone steps.

"Stop right there," Strachan told him harshly. "We know you keep that damned submachine gun in your room. If you take another step towards it I'll put a bullet in your guts."

"We should put a bullet in him anyway." Cameron raised his automatic. He had not been particularly fond of Janis Wallace but he had always disliked the queer. "That's all he's fit for."

"What else can we do with a murderer?" Munro pointed out with cold logic.

"Aye," Strachan agreed. "We can hardly take him to the police. And I'll not see him kill the girl and get away with it. Do it, Hugh."

"I would not advise it, Señor Cameron!"

Strachan whirled and looked into the black eye of a Colt .45. Behind the Colt was Arturo Vincenzi. He too had heard the faint screams and had left his helicopter to investigate.

"I do not know what has happened here," the young Venezuelan said coldly. "But no one will shoot Orlando until he has been given the opportunity to explain."

"Stay out, laddie," Strachan warned him. "We're three guns to your one. And I've another dozen men out there!"

There was a moment of silence. Vincenzi faced the three young Scots and showed no sign of backing down. Then there was a movement at the head of the stairs. Vincenzi did not shift his gaze but the others glanced up.

Cobral had appeared with another automatic in his hand. He wore trousers only, his feet were bare and the tattoo of the striking cobra stood out lividly on his chest. His hair was tousled and obviously he had only just scrambled out of bed. Behind him was Fiona Strachan. Her dark hair was loose and she was still hastily tying up the belt of the dressing gown that covered her nakedness.

"Stop all this foolishness!" Cobral commanded. "We cannot afford to squabble among ourselves. Orlando, come up here and explain."

Savas swallowed hard and then retreated up the stairs. Strachan looked mad enough to shoot him but then Fiona pushed forward to confront her brother.

"Duncan," she ordered angrily. "Put those guns away!"

The situation was confused and the argument began.

The old man had dragged his paralyzed lower limbs over the wet grass of the great hall, and then up over the barrier of paved flagstones that led through the arched doorway in the ruined wall. He fell down the three stone steps into the outer courtyard and lay gasping for breath. Already he was soaked to the skin and the rain lashing down upon his head and shoulders was a driving weight that pushed his face into the muddy grass. He was half frozen and the winds were barbed with ice. The storm was unabated and now he could hear the mighty thunder of the waves that crashed on to the rocks below the castle. He was beginning to wish that he had not chosen such a hellish black night, but it was too late to turn back.

He reached forward with the sore and bloodied talons that were his hands, dug his numb fingers into the sodden grass and dragged himself another few inches. He was aiming for one of the gaps in the crumbling outer wall. Beyond was the steep slope down to the forest and the road. If he could reach the road then there was the vague hope that he might be found by someone from outside the castle at dawn.

He heard the commotion of angry voices that filtered out from within the castle and raised his head to listen. The rain stung viciously at his face and the wind clawed at his hair. He thought the uproar could only mean that he had been missed and that a search would begin. Bitter frustration surged through him and he redoubled his efforts to escape. If only he could get beyond the castle walls there was still hope that in the howling darkness they would fail to find him.

He clutched at the wet grass and heaved with his shoulders. Clutching and heaving, clutching and heaving, and sobbing with pain and anguish, he moved like a burrowing mole through the merciless downpour.

It took Cobral half an hour to restore order and get Savas safely into his room. Then the terrorist commander turned his attention to the disposal of the body. There was more argument but finally with Fiona's help he succeeded in convincing Strachan and his companions that it was best that the body should be removed from the castle and hidden before dawn. Fiona suggested a small but deep loch that was less than a mile away.

Strachan reluctantly agreed. They found raincoats and flashlights and wrapped the body in a blanket. Cobral and Munro lifted Janis with ease and Strachan led the way out into the night.

Cameron went back to the tent, refusing to help and still cursing and mutinous. Vincenzi and Fiona went back up the stairs to stand guard with Savas until Cobral returned.

The old man was clear of the castle and he did not hear the burial party emerge behind him. He was more dead than alive and his whole universe had been reduced to the steep slope of grass and stones that was beneath him. He was deaf and blind and almost without feeling. There was only a last stubborn flicker of will left to drive him on.

Then the inevitable happened and his body started to slide on the wet, slippery incline. He was powerless to stop himself and gathered momentum as he rolled. He cried out in a wild shriek of despair and then his flailing body hit a boulder and he lay helpless.

The cry was heard and torch beams probed the rain-filled darkness to find him. He heard the angry voices of his son and the man they called the Cobra and realized dimly that they were burdened with the dead body of a girl.

Then, instead of the black nightmare, there was black peace as he fainted away.

FOURTEEN

Frank Kasler sat on a hard chair behind a bare table in a bare, grey room. He had collapsed at the ranch house from the combined effects of bourbon and shock and recovered later in a cell. Then they had brought him up here. All that he knew was that he was somewhere inside Houston Police Headquarters, and that he hadn't had a real drink for at least twenty-four hours. His body felt like a wrung-out dishrag. There was nausea in his stomach and a dull ache in his head. His mouth tasted awful.

The door opened and they came in: the big Negro who had been a prisoner at the ranch house, and the man with the grim, rough-hewn face that he had seen briefly at the shattered window. They dragged up chairs and sat down to face him.

"You had enough coffee?" Regan asked. His face didn't change and his voice was toneless.

Kasler nodded dumbly. He had drunk black coffee until he felt that it would spew out of his ears.

"A cigarette?" Regan offered him an opened pack.

"Thanks." Kasler took one with trembling fingers. He held it awkwardly until Johnson leaned forward and snapped flame from a gas lighter under his nose. Kasler sucked smoke and Johnson withdrew. Kasler couldn't look Johnson in the face.

"The men you knew as Rashid and Jemal are both dead," Regan told him in the same flat voice. "The third Arab national, the man who calls himself Sharaf, is alive. But he's not talking. It's gonna take a hammer and a chisel to get his mouth open, and we just might do that if we have to."

Kasler felt as though the smoke had turned to ice in his lungs. He stared into the hard blue eyes.

"Gloria—my wife?"

"She wasn't hurt. Right now she's in a cell downstairs, but she isn't talking either. Quite a tough little woman you've got there, Kasler. I'd say she's got all the backbone for both of you. We could break her but we can't afford the time. That's why you're gonna have to do all the talking."

"But I don't know anything. Those men were friends of Gloria's. They were just staying with us for a few days. If they robbed a bank or something and were hiding out, then it's all news to me."

"That's a poor bluff," Johnson said sadly. "We investigated your hangar and your airplane. We found nine gas cylinders, six of them empty, and the crop-spraying tanks on your Cherokee were all filled up with gas ready for another flight."

"And we've got a chemical warfare expert who is ready to stand up in court and testify that the gas is VX—the type of nerve gas that killed every man aboard two oil rigs out in the Gulf." Regan leaned forward. "If you flew that plane, Kasler, you'll fry!"

"I didn't!" Kasler felt panic rising. "Rashid was the pilot. They took the plane up without me. I didn't know what they were going to do."

"How come three strangers are free to just walk in and use your plane?"

Kasler was sweating and dying for a drink. "I want a lawyer," he said desperately. "I'm not saying any more without a lawyer."

Regan and Johnson exchanged glances. They had already decided that Kasler was the weak link and the

138

quickest source of answers, and they didn't want to waste time.

"Show him," Regan said.

Johnson nodded. He reached inside his coat and took out a photograph which he slid across the bare table in front of Kasler. It was the carefully posed picture of a man, stripped to the waist with his hands resting casually on his hips. The face was dark but handsome, a Latin American face with Spanish eyes and a white-flashing smile. A large striking cobra adorned the bared chest.

"Know him?" Johnson asked.

Kasler gulped, then shook his head. He didn't look up.

Johnson flipped the photograph over. On the back it had been signed with a flourish, *Love from Luis.*

"Your wife knew him," Johnson said. "I found it hidden away with some of her private things."

"I'd say she knew him well," Regan turned the screw. "Gloria is the kind of woman who needs a lot of man, and this looks like the kind of guy who'd need a lot of woman. I'd guess they had a good thing going together."

Kasler turned red, getting mad. "There was nothing!"

"How would you know?" Johnson asked. "You're too dumb to ask what three guys are doing with your airplane. So you're probably too dumb to know what another guy is doing with your wife!"

"A woman don't hide love photos from her husband if she's innocent," Regan said. He guessed shrewdly. "If she got you into this then she's not worth protecting."

Johnson slowly turned the photograph face up again. Kasler stared at it and the cigarette broke up in his twitching fingers. He had suspected Gloria of sleeping with Sharaf. This was new but suddenly it was no surprise. His face and neck flushed hotter with the thought. To hell with them all, he decided. He looked up at Johnson and Regan.

"Okay, I'll tell it all. I don't suppose it matters now anyway."

Regan offered him another cigarette. Johnson lit it. Kasler drew in smoke and began.

"Twelve months ago I crashed my plane. You must know that much. I was washed up without it. Things were real bad. Then this guy Luis came along. He had his wife with him, at least, he said it was his wife. She was an Indian girl named Julia. They said their name was Herrero."

"What brought them to you?"

"The girl, Julia, she had studied here in the US. Gloria made friends with her at university. As far as I can make out they were mixed up with some crazy, left wing political group. Gloria talked a lot about some guy called Trotsky before we were married. I thought that she had settled down and forgotten all that stuff but maybe I was wrong."

"So an old friend of Gloria's brought Luis to the ranch house, go on from there."

"He made me an offer," Kasler said simply. "One hundred thousand dollars paid into my account to buy a new plane, and the only condition was that at certain times it had to be made available to his friends. I couldn't afford to turn it down."

"With a deal like that didn't you ask any questions?"

Kasler shook his head miserably. "I was mostly drunk at the time. The deal was so good that I didn't want to take any chances. Julia and Gloria talked a lot together and I figured that Gloria understood better what was going on. She told me it was okay. She knows a hell of a lot more than I do."

"We'll get back to her," Regan promised him. "But right now you're talking. How many times did you meet Luis?"

"Only once, when the deal was set up." Kasler looked at the photograph and added bitterly. "But Gloria saw him several times, at a hotel somewhere here in Houston. It was all arranged before she brought him to me."

"When did the three Arabs show up?"

"About a month ago. They came in a small truck with those damned cylinders loaded in the back. Julia Herrero was with them, but she only stayed to make the introductions. She was in a big hurry to get away again and Gloria drove her back to Houston. She caught a plane the same night but I don't know where she went."

"Do you know where she is now?"

"No."

"Do you know where we can find Luis?"

"No."

The questions went on for another hour but they learned nothing more. Kasler had nothing left to tell them.

They were ready to start on Gloria for the second time round when Roy Hanson brought in a report. Kasler had been taken back to his cell and Gloria had not yet arrived.

"CIA priority from Langley," Hanson said briefly. "Origin Major Minnelli in Caracas, Venezuela. Marked for your immediate attention, Colonel."

Regan read it through and looked at Johnson.

"All the confirmation we need," he said with satisfaction. "One of Joe's friends has checked out the English-Spanish language school on the Avenida Margarita. There was a stack of literature on guerrilla training and warfare, and copies of a long essay by Cobral entitled *The psychological advantages and political necessity of international terrorism*. There was also a record of the school's students. Three months ago Cobral was teaching Spanish to a mixed class of three Japanese and three Arabs with home addresses in Lebanon."

"So Luis Herrero and Luis Cobral are the same

141

man," Johnson said. "We'd figured that much anyway. We don't know where he is but Julia Herrero is still in Caracas."

"Do you want a flight booked to Venezuela?" Hanson asked.

Regan shook his head. "There's more to this report. The Venezuelan police arrested Julia Herrero yesterday afternoon. They pulled her in on suspicion of being involved with the terrorist group that bombed their oil installations. It looks as though the Peruvian authorities tipped them off when they made a move to get her extradited. She's now in jail at Caracas Police Headquarters, where Minnelli can't reach her and neither would I."

He dropped the report and looked at Hanson.

"Roy, get me on the next flight to New York. I want eight hours stop to sleep and say hello to my wife, and from there on I want to be on the next international flight to London. Cobral isn't on this side of the Atlantic, so he has to be leading the third terror team in England."

FIFTEEN

Steve Regan and Mark Nicolson knew each other well. Two years before two members of an extreme right wing Israeli organization had stopped briefly in London on a deliberately roundabout route from Tel Aviv to New York. Their assassination target had been the PLO leader Yassir Arafat on the occasion of his historic reception at the United Nations. A Counter-Terror warning from the London office had traveled ahead of the intending killers and had given Regan and other CIA and FBI agents the opportunity to intervene before the Israelis could make their move. It was that incident, coupled with an Arab terrorist attack and murders at the US embassy in the Sudan, that had caused the US State Department to decide that it was essential for the United States to become part of the new Counter-Terror network that was already flourishing successfully in Europe. Steve Regan had flown to London and on that occasion had worked for two months with Nicolson and Alexander Gwynne-Vaughan.

Now, twenty-four hours after leaving Houston, Regan found that London and New Scotland Yard had not changed. London was still overhung by grey skies, and the Yard was still a glass-faced white granite tower filled with a communications and monitoring complex of radio, teleprinters and television, a million tons of paperwork and typewriters, and over twenty thousand

143

assorted police officers all laboring over the tangled worlds of crime.

Regan remembered the young detective sergeant who drove him from the airport, and he remembered Harry Stone who was waiting with Nicolson. They made themselves comfortable and the detective sergeant appeared again to leave a pot of coffee.

"We've booked you a room at the Hilton," Nicolson said when the initial welcome was over. He smiled and added, "The IRA bombed it a few months back, but we're hoping that they won't do it again until the redecorations are complete. So you should be safe."

"That's a comfort," Regan said. He poured himself a cup of coffee and then asked after the missing face. "Where's Sir Alexander? I thought he'd be here."

"He's up in Scotland," Nicolson answered. "At the moment we've got every police officer in the northeastern counties engaged in a massive search operation for this terrorist team and their helicopter. Sir Alexander is coordinating all the activity from Inverness, and he's got a special task force of three anti-terrorist teams from the Special Air Services, plus police dog handlers and marksmen, all ready to move as soon as they get the word."

"But so far they haven't got the word?"

Nicolson smiled wryly. "That's about the size of it. The Highlands comprise some very wild and rugged country. There are still vast tracts of mountains and forest where there are no roads, and it's still the last haunt of most of the real wildlife left in the British Isles. There must be a million places where a really determined group could hide out with a helicopter. Our real hope is that we'll be able to intercept when they make another flight. We've got a helicopter information center set up, and the oil companies have been understandably eager to cooperate with advance warning whenever one of their helicopters lifts off the ground. If there's a rogue in the air we should soon know about it."

"How about this girl who lifted the VX gas formula, are there any leads there?"

"A dead end. The name she gave was obviously false. She appeared from nowhere and vanished again." Nicolson paused and then continued. "Our most promising line of enquiry is one that you have started rolling. I've studied your reports about Luis Cobral and the language school he ran as a terrorist cover in Caracas. If you are right and Cobral is involved here then we believe that he is most probably working with a group of Scottish extremists who call themselves the New Scottish Liberation Army. Somewhere there had to be a mutual ground where they could have made their first contact, and that made me wonder whether Cobral might have started out by setting up his usual cover here in England."

"We've been looking for Spanish teachers," Harry Stone explained quietly. "I've had men checking the ad columns in all our newspapers, and the notice boards at universities, colleges, libraries and so forth. We struck lucky at the London School of Economics, which is always a promising source of young revolutionaries. On the board we found a card advertising a tutor of Spanish who called himself Luis Sanchez. He was operating from a flat in Kensington. I called at the flat myself with a detective sergeant. The owner of the flat described Señor Sanchez as a South American gentleman. He rented the flat ten weeks ago and stayed for about six weeks. During that time he received a large number of student-type visitors. Some of them made several visits and presumably an attempt to learn Spanish. A month ago Señor Sanchez disappeared. He left the flat clean."

Regan was showing interest. "The timetable fits," he said. "Three months ago Cobral was coaching three Japs and three Arabs in Caracas. Then he left Venezuela. Julia Herrero took the Japanese team down to

Bozzanos in the Amazon, and then escorted the Arab team to the Kasler ranch in Texas. While she was handling that Cobral must have been in England setting up this end of the operation."

Nicolson nodded agreement. "We've yet to prove that Sanchez was Cobral, but the circumstantial evidence is strong. We've managed to trace a few of the students who paid him a visit. Most of them were clam-mouthed but one girl was willing to talk. It seems that Sanchez tried to seduce her and she took a dim view of the casual way he went about it. She thought that he was insulting. She only attended two of his Spanish lessons, and says that each time he included a lot of inflammatory political talk. Sanchez was left wing, anti-establishment, very clever and very convincing. And he hinted that he approved of violence as a means of reshaping society for the better. It all sounds as though he was inviting kindred spirits to proclaim themselves."

"Then he has to be Cobral," Regan said. "And this should prove it." He showed them the signed photograph that had belonged to Gloria Kasler.

The girl whom Luis Sanchez had insulted was a serious, dark-haired young woman with spectacles named Margaret Robson. Looking at her an hour later in the cramped flat she shared with three other girl students, both Regan and Nicolson could see where Sanchez had miscalculated. Margaret Robson was a stereotype Plain Jane who looked as though she ought to have been grateful when a handsome Latin American showed a sexual interest. But she was sufficiently intelligent to be resentful when there was no parallel approach to her mind.

She held the photograph for less than ten seconds before returning it to Regan.

"Yes," she said positively. "This is Señor Sanchez. I

never saw him without his shirt, but I wouldn't mistake the face."

Regan smiled hopefully now. "Do you know where we can find him now?"

Margaret Robson shook her head. "I haven't seen him since I went to the flat in Kensington. I only went twice. I wanted to learn Spanish but I got the impression that he was more interested in teaching politics. I've told all this to the detective inspector who called yesterday."

"I know we're a nuisance," Nicolson said. "But you've been very helpful and we do appreciate it." He paused and tried a long shot. "Among the other students, was there a girl called Fiona Smith?"

"Your Inspector Stone asked that one and the answer is still no."

Nicolson smiled ruefully. "Any Fionas at all?"

"Not while I was there."

"Were there any Scottish girl students?"

Margaret Robson hesitated. "There was one, a girl named Janis Wallace. She was well-established and very close to Sanchez. I'm sure she was sleeping with him."

"Where can we find her?"

"I don't know, but she was another student at the LSE."

A visit to the London School of Economics revealed that Janis Wallace had left in the middle of a course five weeks before. The school register gave her home address as 25, Argyll Street, Perth.

Nicolson radioed an immediate request to Perthshire CID.

Half an hour later two Scottish detective sergeants were knocking on the door of the Wallace home. The old couple who answered had not seen their errant daughter for the past two months. All they knew was that she had written vaguely of her intention of living with a hippie commune somewhere in Scotland.

The information was flashed back to Nicolson.

Nicolson promptly relayed it north again to the center of the vast Highlands police hunt at Inverness.

SIXTEEN

Cobral saw the police car from his bedroom window. It pulled to a leisurely stop on the main road below the castle. Two young police officers climbed out. They were in uniform but he noted that they carried no rank. It was midmorning and the weather was good. The waves slapped on the rocks below the cliffs and the wind blew cold from the sea. The castle walls looked stark and dramatic against a blue-grey sky. The two policemen stared up for a moment, and then began the long climb up the steep path to the ruined gateway. They appeared to be in no hurry.

Fiona moved up by Cobral's side. She saw the car and the two men and her body stiffened.

"Don't panic," Cobral told her calmly. "In Venezuela I became accustomed to establishment pigs calling at my home. It is probably routine harassment."

There was a sharp knock on the door. Cobral called an invitation and Savas came in. For the past two days he had not moved outside his room without his submachine gun slung over one shoulder, and now he held the weapon ready in his hands. Vincenzi was behind him.

"We stay out of sight," Cobral instructed. "This is something that Duncan will have to handle."

"I'd better go down and help him," Fiona decided. "He's stupid enough to make a right mess of it if he's left on his own."

Cobral nodded approval. Fiona wore a red sweater

and a dark skirt, and she paused to pull on a trendy, fur-trimmed coat before she hurried out. Savas and Vincenzi came into the room and joined Cobral at the window. They waited and watched.

As she passed through the great hall Fiona found Cameron and Munro handing out automatic rifles and ammunition. The haul from a robbery at an army camp months before.

"Put those bloody things away," she told them angrily. "We're not starting the war on our own territory."

Cameron opened his mouth for a rude retort but Fiona had no time to stop and listen. She swept on and left him bristling, and hoped that they had enough sense to obey. She passed through the archway and hurried across the grassed courtyard. Duncan was waiting in the gap in the outer walls where the gates had once been. He looked back as she approached, his face very fierce and grim behind his black beard.

"For God's sake relax," Fiona said. "Stop trying to look like the Chief of the Clans besieged in his stronghold."

Strachan laughed, and when the two policemen reached them he was still smiling.

"It's a long haul," Constable Dave Mackinnon said breathlessly. He was the spokesman of the two, his driver being of a more taciturn nature.

"It is that," Strachan agreed. "But you didn't make it just to pay your fifty pence and see the ancestral home. What is it that you want?"

"Mr. Duncan Strachan, isn't it?" Mackinnon gave him a speculative look and received a nod. "We understand that you're running some kind of a hippie commune up here?"

"And what if I am? My choice of friends is my own business."

"No offense meant," Mackinnon said quickly.

"Have you come to join us?" Fiona smiled at him sweetly.

"Not exactly—we're looking for a girl."

"Aren't we all!" Strachan grinned and the undercurrent of tension passed.

"This one is missing from home," Mackinnon told them. "Her family in Perth haven't heard from her in five weeks and they're beginning to get worried. All they know is that she's living with a hippie commune rather like this one. Her name is Janis Wallace."

Duncan Strachan felt the tension surge within him. His nerves were suddenly taut and his body rigid. He stared into the inquiring eyes beneath the police officer's peaked cap and his mouth was dry.

"We've no girl by that name here," Fiona said. Her smile was strained and a muscle twitched in her cheek.

"Perhaps you know her by another name," Mackinnon said hopefully. "She's a tall, thin girl. Long blonde hair, although she could have had it cut short by now. Green eyes. She's in her early twenties."

"No," Strachan said with an effort. "We've got no one like that."

"The only blonde girls in our group are both short and chubby," Fiona added. She smiled helpfully. "We've heard that there's another commune living in an old shooting lodge near Loch Naver and there's a smaller group in a farmhouse in Wester Ross. You could try those. As far as I know they are the only other communes in the Highlands."

Mackinnon hesitated. His silent partner stared unsmiling at Strachan and the black-bearded Scot felt definitely uncomfortable.

"Thanks for your help," Mackinnon said at last. "We'll make a note of those other communes."

Both police officers saluted politely and then they turned away.

* * *

151

Hamish Strachan had been returned to his room in the west wing and the door had been locked. When he had recovered consciousness after his ordeal he had found that Fiona had bandaged his hands and that Duncan was waiting beside him. He remembered vaguely that Duncan and Cobral had been arguing violently in the storm before he had passed out. Cobral had wanted him killed, but Duncan had stood in the way.

After seeing the old man in such a pitiful condition Duncan had at last felt that he owed his father an explanation of what was happening, and it had proved a painful experience for both of them. The Earl was already horrified by what his children were doing, and now even more so by the reasons behind it.

"You were the one who taught me that the English Crown had no moral right to rule over Scotland," Duncan had told him. "When I was a child at your knee you told me stories about the clans and our past kinsmen, and the old glories of Strachan Castle. You told me how our clansmen fought with Robert the Bruce when we defeated the English at Bannockburn. You told me that an Earl of Strachan died with James the Fourth when the clansmen fell in their hundreds to the arrows of the English archers at Flodden. And you told me that there were Strachan clansmen in the last fierce charge of the highland swordsmen at Culloden, where the forces of Bonnie Prince Charlie were put to route.

"Father I'm still fighting for Scotland's independence! You taught me that only the strongest clan chief could be Chief of the Clans. And only the Chief of the Clans has a true right to rule over the Highlands!"

"That was only history," the old man said wretchedly. "Old stories to amuse a child. You can't bring back the past."

"No, but I can win a new future."

"What you're doing is simple murder and destruction. It's black-hearted and evil."

"It's the modern way to win a war of independence.

152

You can still believe in the nobility of clan blood, but you can't win Scotland with a sword!"

"Does Fiona think like this?"

"Fiona is a bloody socialist," Duncan said scornfully. "She thinks she's using me for Cobral and his dreams of world revolution. Cobral thinks he is using me. But I'm my own man, and my cause is Scotland."

"You're insane," the old man cried. "Can't you see that they *are* using you?"

They had argued bitterly until dawn.

Now the old man had watched the two police officers toiling up the slope to the castle and the quarrel with Duncan was still in his mind. Somehow his own simple pride in his forbears had led his son into terrorism and he felt a terrible burden of responsibility. He had seen briefly the face of a dead girl and he knew instinctively that she was not the first who had been murdered. He saw the two police officers pass out of sight beneath the castle walls and wondered desperately how he could alert them.

The red scarf that was wrapped around his throat suggested an answer. He pulled it off and then hacked it into two halves with a blunt knife from his breakfast tray. Next he propelled his chair over to the bed and tore off a white sheet. With four pins he fixed the two halves of the scarf in a red cross on a square of the white sheet. Then he wheeled himself back to the window.

He saw the two police officers descending the slope again to their car. He held his signal up to the window and prayed that one of them would glance back and see it.

Neither man looked back. They climbed into their car and drove away.

The old man crumpled up the flag. He was utterly dejected and there was nothing left but to throw it into a corner.

* * *

Duncan and Fiona returned to the great hall. Cameron and the others were waiting for them beside the tent.

"What did they want?" Cameron asked harshly.

"They were looking for Janis," Fiona said bluntly.

There were shocked faces around the circle. The death of Janis Wallace had had a traumatic effect, and now it was as though her ghost had suddenly walked.

"Why should they want Janis?"

"Have they found her body?"

"They couldn't find it," Strachan snapped. "We sank it in the deepest part of the loch."

"Perhaps it floated to the surface again."

"I tied a bloody great iron grating to her legs." Munro was baffled but sure of himself. "It carried her straight to the bottom."

"Perhaps you didn't tie it tight enough."

"I know how to tie a knot, and the rope was strong. It couldn't have come unfastened."

"Then why are the police asking questions about Janis?" Cameron demanded.

The raised voices became heated and then Cobral appeared from the west wing. Vincenzi and Savas were at his heels. They joined the larger group and Cobral aimed his terse question at Fiona.

"What has happened?"

She told him and his face became grim.

"Did they give any reason for wanting the girl?"

"Only that she's been reported as missing from home. They said that her family in Perth were worried."

"So we cannot be sure that they know she is dead?"

"They can't know," Strachan insisted.

"They must know." Cameron was equally positive. "The pigs were spying, and obviously all they would tell us would be a pack of lies."

Cobral frowned, thinking back to the night when

154

Janis Wallace had died. "Nobody saw us in the storm, the night was so black and the rain so heavy that we could barely see each other. And I am also sure the body was properly weighted. I watched Señor Munro tie the knots. I do not think it is possible the police can know the girl is dead."

"Then why were they here?"

"It's all the fault of yon weird one. If he hadn't murdered the lass—"

"Enough of this!" Cobral's voice was incensed. "The girl deliberately tormented Orlando, and she was drunk. Her death was a regrettable accident. We have established these facts and it is pointless to dwell upon them. We cannot afford to quarrel among ourselves."

"Maybe." Cameron was belligerent. "But I think it's time we moved out. Now that the police are taking an interest in the commune it's no longer a safe cover. The castle is too dangerous for us to stay."

"Hugh may be right." Strachan faced Cobral. "And if you haven't got the guts to make another flight in the helicopter then there's no need for us to take the risk."

"It is not a question of guts," Vincenzi said coldly. "But a matter of timing and commonsense."

"Even so we've delayed enough for your operation. Our ultimatum has expired and our campaign to attack the onshore oil industry is overdue. Scotland's oil is already flowing south into England and that has got to stop. Also I've been thinking that we can use a couple of those VX gas cylinders in conjunction with conventional bombs. If we blow them up in London and Edinburgh there'll be hell to pay. Whitehall will have to start listening to us then."

"Let Luis make the decisions." Fiona shouted at him. "It's the world revolution that is important and Luis knows what is right. He has all the experience."

"Wait, wait!" Cobral raised both hands in the gesture of a placating orator. He could see that the situa-

155

tion was about to explode beyond his control and an open clash between brother and sister had to be averted.

"Fiona, perhaps Duncan is right. We do not know why the pigs paid us a visit, but the fact that they have done so must indicate that the castle is under suspicion. The wise course is to leave, and considering the friction that exists between our two parties it may be best to separate."

"But, Luis, all your plans?"

Cobral smiled calmly. "I have not told you yet, but Arturo and I have planned another flight for today."

There was silence. He had all their attention now and they were willing to listen.

"This will be our last flight over the North Sea," Cobral continued. "It would be foolish to make identical attacks until we are caught, and if this flight is successful it will be the psychological terror blow that will halt all North Sea oil production. No man will want to risk his life by continued working on an offshore oil rig. Afterwards we must devise new ideas for using the remaining nerve gas. Perhaps Duncan's suggestion is the right one. I will give it my consideration."

"But the oil rigs are still under heavy guard," Fiona protested. "And they haven't lifted the intensified naval and air patrols."

"There is one rig that is not under guard," Cobral contradicted. "And hopefully one that has not yet been included in the pattern of regular patrols." He paused. "This is the rig that I have been waiting for. I refer to Colossus Three."

The circle of faces was blank. Then Munro said slowly:

"Colossus Three? Isn't that the new rig they've just launched from Stavanger in Norway?"

Cobral nodded. "The biggest oil drilling platform in the world, señors. Four hundred thousand tons in weight and over nine hundred feet high. It was launched from Stavanger four days ago and is now being towed to its drilling position in the British sector of the North Sea by a fleet of six powerful, deepsea tug-ships. I calculate that it has now left the Norwegian sector and is within our operational range."

"They will be moving very slowly," Vincenzi said. "Nothing could be more vulnerable."

"Can you imagine it, señors?" Cobral was again smiling. "We will pass over the line of tug-ships and release the nerve gas. There will be six death ships full of corpses, and the most monstrous oil platform ever built, all hopelessly adrift in the crowded sea lanes of the North Sea. Perhaps they will collide with other rigs, or other vessels. We will have caused the greatest havoc in maritime history."

SEVENTEEN

The Counter-Terror Hercules landed at Inverness Airport at twelve noon. As the great transport aircraft eased to a stop the nose ramp came down and from its cavernous belly were disgorged two Land Rovers fitted with rocket side launchers and two armoured cars fitted with light machine guns. A small fleet of conventional Land Rovers sped up to the aircraft to absorb the police and army marksmen, the additional dog handling teams and the bomb disposal experts who made up the flying task force, and within minutes the whole convoy was mobile. They headed north along the tortuous, winding A9 road that followed the northeastern coastline of Scotland.

Steve Regan and Mark Nicolson were also on board the Hercules, but here they parted company with the convoy. A large Sea King anti-submarine and commando assault helicopter was waiting to whirl them ahead of the main force. The Sea King flew a direct line over the wild grey firths of Moray and Dornoch and lowered them twenty-five minutes later on to a flat cliff top beside the small town of Rosskirk on the Caithness coast.

Three more Sea Kings were standing by, and the hand-picked men of the Special Air Services who formed Britain's elite anti-terrorist spearhead were waiting ready for action.

A police car rushed Regan and Nicolson into Rosskirk where Alexander Gwynne-Vaughan had now set up his forward command post in the local police station.

Police Constable Dave Mackinnon was trying hard not to be overawed by the vast hornet's-nest of activity that his report had disturbed. The circle of faces that surrounded him were mostly hard and uncompromising, but his voice remained calm and steady as he told his story for the twentieth time for the benefit of Regan and Nicolson.

"I saw the signal flag in the rear-view mirror as we were driving away from the castle. I help a friend of mine to sail a small boat in my spare time so I've learned something about flags. At sea a red cross on a white background means. *I require assistance!*"

"Do you have any idea who could have been holding up the signal?" Nicolson asked.

"At a guess I would say it had to be the Earl of Strachan himself. Duncan and Fiona came to the gate and if they are covering up then all of the hippie people they've invited to the castle must be involved. Old Hamish would be the only odd man out. His wife died six months ago and since then Fiona is supposed to have been looking after her father."

Regan noted the girl's name and exchanged glances with Nicolson. It wasn't conclusive proof but it was another pointer.

"How did they react when you asked about Janis Wallace?" Regan demanded.

"They were shocked." Mackinnon was puzzled but sure of his facts. "Duncan went pale behind his beard, and Fiona looked as though the sky had fallen on to her head. I'm sure the Wallace girl must have been there, but why the very mention of her name should petrify the two of them is something I don't understand."

"What makes you so sure that Janis Wallace is at the castle?"

"I'm sure because I know Fiona Strachan lied. She told us that the only blonde girls at the castle were both short and chubby, but I've seen a tall, thin blonde girl with them when the hippies have been here in Rosskirk to buy food and wine."

"You're observant," Nicolson approved. "Can you describe any of the others who are living up at the castle?"

"I know Duncan and Fiona well enough, but you already have their descriptions. The others are a scruffy looking lot, all beads and jeans and shaggy coats. One lad stands out though, he's big with a bright red beard, and always wears a kilt with the Cameron tartan."

Nicolson pulled a batch of photographs from his inside pocket, thumbed through them rapidly and selected one to show to Mackinnon. The young constable nodded affirmative. Nicolson showed the photograph briefly to Regan.

"His name is Hugh Cameron. He's one of the political thugs with a Scottish background whom we haven't been able to find."

"This clinches it?"

Nicolson nodded. "I'd say that either Cameron or Duncan Strachan will prove to be our Chief of the Clans."

"I'm inclined to agree," Alexander Gwynne-Vaughan said calmly. "That's why I propose to launch an immediate assault upon Strachan Castle. If we are right and it is the stronghold of the New Scottish Liberation Army then we can expect armed resistance. We cannot afford to let them use any nerve gas they may have left, and a surprise attack should enable us to occupy the castle with the least number of casualties."

"I'd like to come along," Regan said.

Gwynne-Vaughan smiled. "We'll be glad to have you, Colonel. After the Amazon and Texas it would be most unsporting to deprive you of your hat-trick."

After the Hiller had taken flight and disappeared over the sullen grey waste of the North Sea, Strachan called his tattered army together for a council of war in the drawing room of the castle. He stood behind a table on which was pinned a large scale map of Scotland with every aspect of the onshore oil industry clearly marked. On the wall behind him, between the noble heads of two magnificent red stags, a shield on crossed Highland swords bore the Strachan coat of arms.

"It's time for us to move our HQ," he told them firmly. "The police may have found Janis's body or they may not, but they were not satisfied. They'll be back, but we shall be gone."

There were nods of agreement. Only Fiona stood tight-lipped and registering disapproval, but she said nothing.

"Fiona and I will stay here until the return of the helicopter," Strachan continued. "We'll help to get it under cover but what the Cobra does then is his own business."

"Aye, and good luck to him," Cameron said. "I've nothing against the Cobra. It's the other one I could strangle."

"Forget that, there are more important things. Hugh you'll take one party and the bulk of our equipment, including the remaining VX cylinders. Get them to our prepared base in Glen Crief. From there you can strike south at the oil terminal at Grangemouth."

Cameron smiled fiercely.

"Bruce, you'll take a party of three to the safe house in Peterhead. I'll join you there later."

"We all know what to do," Munro acknowledged. "We've discussed tactics often enough."

"When?" Cameron asked. "That's all we have to decide."

"Midnight, two nights from now," Strachan said. "When both ends of the pipeline are wrecked we'll withdraw to Glen Crief. From there we are in a good position to strike at the electricity power pylons and radio masts we've selected as secondary targets."

162

"It's all been done before," Fiona said wearily.

"Isolated attacks at random by the Tartan Army," Strachan qualified. "But we're going to wage a widespread and determined guerrilla war over the whole face of Scotland. When they see what is happening the other underground groups will fall into line and give us support. All it needs is the right organization and leadership, and we can make Scotland unprofitable and untenable to the English."

"They'll have two choices," Cameron said with satisfaction. "Grant independence to Scotland or face another Northern Ireland. And I don't think they could face a repeat of the events in——"

He broke off as they heard the whirling sound of rotor blades over the North Sea.

"They're coming back." Strachan looked puzzled but only faintly alarmed. "They must have hit trouble."

Fiona was listening more intently. "That's not the Hiller," she exclaimed. "The engine note is more powerful. And there's more than one!"

Three of the big Sea Kings came up from the tumbled grey horizons of the North Sea. The fourth swept low over the black forest of firs on the landward side. As the engines thundered overhead the colonies of gulls and terns shrieked and fled from the spray-wet rocks and cliffs. Their white-winged panic mirrored the frenzy of activity within the castle walls.

The armored cars, the rocket-equipped Land Rovers and the convoy of specialists appeared moving at full speed on the road below.

Steve Regan crouched in the open doorway of the fourth Sea King with a borrowed automatic rifle in his hands. The dark crowns of the fir trees flashed past dangerously close beneath him but his eyes were fixed ahead. He saw the other three helicopters closing in fast. One hovered over the highest point of the sprawling, grey-stone ruins, directly above the only wing that looked solid enough to be habitable. Two and Three were landing outside the outer walls on either side.

. The fourth Sea King was aiming for the central courtyard, within the great, jagged jawbone. As it hovered prior to settling down Strachan, Cameron and two others ran across the great hall and ducked into the archway that had once been the main doorway. From this defensive position they opened fire with hastily distributed automatic weapons.

The Sea King was forced to retreat. Regan fired a burst at the archway but the curve of the fuselage blocked his aim. As the Sea King banked to the left he was almost thrown through the open doorway, but Mark Nicolson's hand clamped hard on his shoulder and hauled him back.

The helicopter lifted easily over the outer wall and then dropped again to hover only a few feet above the grassy slope. Regan jumped out. Nicolson landed beside him. As they ran forward to the main gateway a sergeant and five commandos of the SAS surged at their heels. Two of the men restrained savage but highly disciplined Alsatian dogs.

Regan and Nicolson reached the gateway gap together, flattening themselves against the wind-scoured stonework on either side. On the opposite side of the courtyard Strachan and his terrorists let rip another burst of automatic fire from the great hall doorway. Chips of granite splintered above their heads. Regan answered the shots. The SAS men diving flat behind him followed his example.

Nicolson had a Smith & Wesson .38 automatic gripped in his right fist but he didn't bother to use it. He looked up and saw that the men from the Number One SAS unit had already dropped on to the upper battlements of the castle and were disappearing inside. The men from Unit Two were pouring through a gap in the outer wall to his left, while the men from Unit Three were scrambling over the fallen masonry blocks in a partially blocked gap to his right.

Nicolson thumbed the speech button of the two-way radio in his left hand. "Ground Control to units One and Two," he snapped tersely. "Close in on that archway while we give you covering fire."

There was no verbal answer. Each of the tough young paratroop lieutenants in command had his radio clipped to the breast pocket of his flak jacket. They heard and obeyed.

Mercilessly accurate streams of automatic fire from Regan and Unit Four raked the archway to the great hall. Strachan felt a violent blow in his left arm as he dived for cover. When he looked at the arm he saw that there was now a leaking red hole drilled through the muscle. One of his companions lay dead in the archway. Cameron and the third man were beside him.

"Back into the castle," Strachan ordered.

Nicolson saw them retreat.

"Cease fire," he snapped. "Unleash the dogs."

The two dog handlers slipped the chains. The black Alsatians streaked forward in a speed-blur of fur and fangs.

Cameron glanced back over his shoulder and saw the dogs hurtling through the archway. He bellowed a warning and twisted with his rifle. The first dog leaped at his chest and knocked him flying, its white jaws crunching over his right wrist. Strachan turned, trying to bring up his own rifle. His wounded arm had gone numb and the response was too slow. The second Alsatian leaped.

Fiona Strachan stepped out of the doorway to the castle. Among terrorist ranks the female was more deadly than the male, as the world had learned repeatedly to its cost. She held a Sterling 9mm submachine gun, and as her brother slipped and fell on the wet grass she cut the dog to ribbons in midair.

Two of her companions ran out to help Strachan to

his feet. Fiona moved out beside them to shoot the dog that was savaging Cameron. She succeeded, but then all hell broke loose as all three SAS units coverged in the main hall archway.

Regan went straight for the top of the wall that divided the great hall from the courtyard. It was an easy scramble up a slope of rubble and as he threw himself flat he could see three dead terrorists and two dead dogs sprawled below. Fiona and Strachan had retreated inside the castle. Cameron was still staggering toward the doorway.

A live terrorist was always useful and Regan knew that the red-bearded man in the distinctive kilt was one of the leaders. He fired one careful shot and Cameron tumbled into a heap with his legs cut from beneath him. The bullet had gone straight through his thigh.

Nicolson crouched in the great hall doorway with the grim-faced paratroop lieutenants on either side. Again he used his radio.

"Ground Control to Unit One. The terrorists are now all inside the west wing."

"Unit One to Ground Control." The steel voice of the lieutenant-colonel in command was precise and toneless. "We are mopping up as we approach ground level. Stand by and we'll send them out again with their hands up."

The New Scottish Liberation Army made its last stand in the drawing room. Fiona had helped Strachan there, rallying three more terrorists around her. Then Munro joined them with two survivors from the group of six he had tried to lead up to the battlements.

"The bastards are inside the castle," Munro cursed bitterly. "It's bloody hopeless."

"We'll fight on!" Fiona vowed, and there was the light of madness in her eyes. She had forgotten her quarrel with Duncan now and intended that they would die together. If they could not be victorious in battle then at least they would be martyrs in death, an inspiration for other world revolutionaries.

A magnified voice boomed at them from the stone hollows of the corridors outside.

"Your position is hopeless. Throw down your weapons and walk out with your hands above your heads."

"Sassenach bastards!" Fiona screamed. She ran into the doorway and blazed away in the direction of the voice with her submachine gun.

There was a dull clunk and then a metallic skimming noise as a hand grenade rolled up to her feet. Fiona backed away and then dived for cover behind the table.

The grenade exploded. A steel fragment killed one man outright and the blast sent the others flying. Fiona was slammed against the far wall. Her head cracked and she fell full length.

Strachan hauled himself slowly and painfully to his feet. He was dazed and weakening from loss of blood. Smoke and dust had a blinding, abrasive effect on his eyes. He had dropped his automatic rifle but his left arm was now dead and he could not have used it anyway. He was between the two stag's heads that flanked the Strachan coat of arms and he reached up his right hand to draw one of the highland swords from behind the shield.

It was over. He knew that now he would not live to rebuild Strachan Castle, or to see the free and independent Scotland that was his dream. In their last argument his father had been right about so many things, but at least one of his old stories would be proved wrong. The last highlander to fall in a wild sword charge for freedom had not died at Culloden.

He saw that his remaining friends were seeking escape. Munro stood undecided with an empty rifle.

"Stand with me, Bruce!" He offered the second sword.

167

Munro stared at him blankly. His chest was heaving and there was blood on his face. He was a fighter but not a martyr. He shook his head.

Figures filled the shattered doorway, armed men with bleak, careful faces, steel helmets and flak jackets. Strachan launched himself across the drawing room, the tip of his sword blade aimed in a desperate lunge for the throat of the leading man with the rank tabs of a lieutenant colonel on his shoulders.

"For Scotland!"

The last bull roar was drowned by a burst of automatic fire. Bullets crashed into his chest and the charge fell short. The Chief of the Clans died with the sword hilt still locked in his hand.

An organized search of the castle quickly revealed the dungeon laboratory where the VX nerve gas had been produced. Nicolson ordered the underground rooms sealed and a guard placed over them until they could be examined by scientists from Porton Down. One of the paratroop lieutenants reported that a small helicopter had been kept in the stables. His unit had noted the tire marks and oil drips where it had been standing. Then Hamish Strachan was brought down and was able to tell them that Cobral and his two companions had taken flight in the Hiller only an hour before.

Nicolson approached Fiona Strachan who was standing under guard with the other survivors of the NSLA. There was dust and dirt in her hair and a livid bruise above her left eye. She glared at him hatefully.

"We want Luis Cobral," Nicolson told her. "Where has he gone with the helicopter?"

He saw her lips move and guessed at what was coming. He ducked neatly to avoid the mouthful of spit she aimed at his face and then moved away. He knew that he would get nothing more out of Fiona Strachan.

He began to question the other prisoners but found them all equally sullen. No one would answer and he

168

felt frustration. He was sure that Cobral had set out to attack another oil rig and already he had alerted all the offshore protection patrols, but there were more than sixty possible targets scattered over the whole of the North Sea.

Then Steve Regan appeared from the castle, moving fast.

"We've found the room that Cobral must have used," he told Nicolson briefly. "He's been keeping recent newspapers and making calculations on a chart. It looks as though he's been tracking the movement of a new rig they've just launched from Norway. It's a monster they've called Colossus Three."

EIGHTEEN

After two and a half hours of flying the Hiller was two hundred miles out in the North Sea when Cobral finally spotted his target. Colossus Three rose out of the grey waves on three gigantic legs, a skyscraper platform that was taller than the Rockefeller Center in New York. The rig was a magnificent triumph of engineering, more awe-inspiring than a pyramid or a floating cathedral. It outweighed the biggest ocean liners ever built and made the six tugboats spread out before it on a fan pattern of churned white wake look like miniature toys.

Cobral thought that the only technological comparison would be a moon rocket. Against a blue-grey sky piled with darkening cumulus cloud it was starkly beautiful, and the cost of its construction had been astronomical.

Cobral felt a fleeting moment of admiration for the achievement, but he determined to destroy it. Colossus Three represented the blind capitalist system that filled him with fury. It was the system that supported dictatorship and economic strangleholds over the masses; a system that poured its wealth and energies into projects such as this, simply to recycle more wealth and energy for the few, while the Third World starved in its slums and shanties.

Even without the directive from Terror Incorporated, Cobral would still have sought the destruction of Colossus Three.

There were four English and two Norwegian tugs engaged in the long tow. On the left flank of the slow-steaming half circle was *Bulldog*, then *Black Knight*, *Dundee Lass*, *Annika*, *Boxer* and on the right flank *Skagerrak*. They had a combined eighty thousand horsepower but with every towline taut they could only crawl forward at a snail's pace.

Cobral pointed down at *Bulldog*. "We will attack from the left flank and release the gas over the bridge of every ship in turn."

Vincenzi nodded and turned the helicopter away in a wide sweep that would bring them back on Cobral's chosen attack path from the north. His hands were steady on the controls but there was tension and elation within him. It had taken thousands of men and millions of dollars to design and build Colossus Three, but their years of labor would be destroyed by three men in a matter of seconds. He felt proud to be a part of this. It was a blow for the underprivileged of the world, a new beginning for the revolutionary cause that had been temporarily lost in the jungles of Venezuela.

Savas leaned forward behind them. His bright eyes were eager and his tongue licked deliciously across his lips. He held his submachine gun tightly and wished that it was bullets and not nerve gas that was about to bring death to the ships below. Killing made him feel a man, and also it was something he could share with Luis that no woman had ever shared.

The Hiller made its turn and came back under the huge, dwarfing shadow of Colossus Three, Vincenzi took them low over the raised bridge of *Bulldog* and they saw anxious faces staring up from the wheelhouse windows. Cobral released a cloud of nerve gas as they passed overhead.

All the escort vessels had been forewarned by radio and the crews had made desperate efforts to seal themselves inside their doomed ships. The minute droplets of VX penetrated through the ventilation system and the officers and men aboard *Bulldog* began to choke and writhe as agony and nausea overtook them.

The Hiller whirled on to the next ship in the line. *Black Knight* was mounting the crest of a wave as more gas was puffed out in an invisible cloud over her bows.

Bulldog was already veering off course as her helmsman slumped dead over the spokes of the wheel.

The first Sea King came out of the western sky with its rotor blades thundering at maximum revolutions. Apart from the pilot and co-pilot only Regan and Nicolson were aboard. The remaining Sea Kings were minutes behind with their full complements of men, but in order to get every last thrust of speed from the leading machine Nicolson had decided that it would fly with the lightest possible load.

"There!" Regan snapped, as the towering shape of the rig loomed like some vast steel, high-altitude island against the clouds and above the sea. It looked invincible, but in the same moment they saw the smaller helicopter making its run over the wide-spread line of white bow waves that marked the positions of the tugboats.

"Intercept," Nicolson said sharply to the pilot. "Head them off, but keep them on our left flank."

The pilot nodded understanding and the Sea King swooped. Nicolson and Regan ran back and heaved open the left-side door of the fuselage. Regan still had his borrowed automatic rifle and he crouched and braced himself as Nicolson took another restraining grip on his shoulder.

The Hiller was within seconds of passing over *Dundee Lass* when Vincenzi realized abruptly that they were not alone in the sky. He heard the beat of rotors more powerful than his own and glanced up to see the Sea King descending upon them like an avenging hawk about to pounce on a sparrow. He made a fast turn towards the rig but then a burst of automatic fire from the

173

open doorway of the Sea King shattered the perspex bubble of the cockpit.

Vincenzi saw his left hand jerked away from the control column as something solid plucked at his left arm. In the same moment there was a driving pain beneath his right ribs.

Cobral still had his eyes on the bridge of *Dundee Lass* when he felt the helicopter lurch. The crash of gunfire, the explosion of perspex, and the spurt of red blood that drenched his shirtfront from the severed artery in Vincenzi's arm, all came as a total shock.

From behind them Savas was cursing with rage. He thrust the snout of his submachine gun over Vincenzi's shoulder and fired back at the Sea King as it swept past.

Vincenzi was fighting to control the Hiller. They had swerved towards the flat-topped steel mountain of the oil rig and for a moment it seemed that they must be dashed to pieces against the monstrous girth of the foremost leg. Then he succeeded in tilting the helicopter away. They zig-zagged wildly over the heaving seas and again approached the line of tugboats.

"Hold her steady," Cobral shouted desperately as the straining shape of the Norwegian tug *Annika* rushed up to meet them. His hand was on the gas release lever but again he was thwarted.

The Sea King came back to head them off and again there was a vicious exchange of gunfire between the two machines.

Cobral was still shouting and cursing but Vincenzi was no longer listening. The submachine gun reverberating so close to his eardrums had deafened him and he was losing blood and consciousness fast. He knew that he could not out-fly the bigger and faster Sea King, that their mission had failed and there was no escape.

Vincenzi had a dying choice. He could dive the Hiller into the sea, or he could attempt to crashland on the helicopter landing pad on Colossus Three. The prospect of drowning in the icy grey waters of this sullen and

174

alien ocean was still not attractive, and so he used the last of his strength to pull back the control column.

The Hiller lifted slowly and painfully. It climbed like a sick bird with tired wings. When it finally reached the level of the oil rig platform Vincenzi was on the brink of death. His life blood was gushing from the cut artery and the deep wound in his side. His eyes were glazing and he saw the landing pad through a film of red.

Cobral and Savas could only sit frozen, hypnotized by helplessness and fear.

Vincenzi pushed the control column. The helicopter slid forward and down. The landing pad slammed up at them. Cobral and Savas braced themselves for the impact. Vincenzi switched off his engine and his hands became still. His blood stopped flowing and his head flopped forward, his chin sagging on to his chest. The Hiller dropped like a dead gamebird full of shot, a solid, devastating crash.

Cobral felt as though he was being whirled around inside a cement mixer that was full of churning steel and glass. He was dazed and bruised and pain stabbed him from every angle. There was a terrible grinding noise and he sensed that the helicopter was sliding across the landing pad. He was afraid of fire and he was afraid of the long drop into the sea.

He struggled to open the door, fearing that it was buckled. The strength of desperation filled his arms and then the door slid back. He looked to Vincenzi but realized that his friend was dead. In the same second he became aware that the wrecked helicopter was tottering on the very edge of the landing pad. Sparks were flashing from the shattered control panel and although he had not yet smelled leaking fuel oil the fire fear flooded his brain.

He scrambled out and ran for safety. Vaguely he was aware that Orlando had also struggled clear and was running beside him. Men from the caretaker crew of the oil rig were hurrying up but Cobral drew his automatic and they fell back. Savas was still hugging his precious submachine gun to his chest.

The two terrorists ran down the companionway to the next deck, seeking cover.

Behind them the Sea King was hovering and settling down.

Regan and Nicolson had watched the Hiller crash with fear in their hearts.

"If the VX tanks are ruptured then every man on that rig is dead," Regan said hoarsely.

Nicolson nodded but said nothing. Later he realized that he had been holding his breath.

Regan had the silver protection suit he had worn in the Gulf and in the Amazon in a briefcase beside him. On this job he had carried it everywhere, determined that he would only return it to Freeman when the case was closed. Now he felt a panic temptation to put the suit on but he held it back.

They saw the crumpled Hiller slide across the helicopter landing pad below and balance precariously on the edge. Then they saw Cobral and Savas emerge from the cabin and run back across the pad. A handful of oilmen from the rig's skeleton crew reached the scene in the same moment, stepping hastily aside to let the two armed men dash past. No one had yet collapsed or started to writhe in agony.

"The VX tanks must be intact," Nicolson decided.

Regan agreed. "It's snake-killing time," he said grimly.

Nicolson gave the order and their pilot eased the Sea King down towards the landing pad of the giant rig. There was plenty of room for two helicopters to park side by side but even so they stayed as far away from the crashed Hiller as possible. It was still a fire and explosion risk. The Sea King's wheels touched the landing pad for seconds only as Regan and Nicolson jumped out, and then it soared away again.

Regan had already fitted a full magazine to his automatic rifle and Nicolson had his Smith & Wesson .38 in his hand. They sprinted forward to the point where Cobral and Savas had vanished from view. Looking down, a series of connecting companionways zig-zagged past the layers of accommodation decks to the drilling platform sixty feet below. On this level was a vast maze of pipe racks, winches, pumps and other machinery, including the rotary table and kelly that still awaited the derrick tower that would be welded into place after the huge rig had been positioned and sunk to her working level. The superstructure itself contained dining rooms, galleys, television rooms, a cinema and all the amenities of an ocean liner. Colossus Three offered a thousand places to hide and miles of corridors and rooms to be searched.

Cobral and Savas had disappeared.

The two Counter-Terror men hesitated. Then one of the rig crew moved up to Regan's elbow.

"They went down to main deck level," he offered. "Then I lost sight of them."

"Thanks," Regan said. He looked to Nicolson. "I'll take port side, you take starboard."

"Agreed." Nicolson patted his radio. "Keep in touch."

Regan nodded and raced along the railed gangway to the port companionways. Nicolson started down the steel steps at his feet. Below them the rig was empty of life and movement. They didn't know whether the two terrorists had sought refuge inside the superstructure, or whether they were waiting in ambush somewhere in the jungle of racks and machinery.

They descended the separate companionways fast, crouching and taking advantage of every scrap of cover.

Cobral and Savas had separated, although each had expected the other to follow. Cobral had not gone all the way to the main deck but had burst into the radio

177

shack on the deck level above. He had recognized it by the mast antenna and a radio transmitter was always a useful capture. It offered the prospect of further ultimatums, and perhaps a ransom demand for freedom if he could seize a hostage. A startled radio operator jumped to his feet as the door was kicked open, but Cobral smashed him senseless with a sweeping blow of the automatic that was gripped in his right fist. If the hostage idea had not been forming in his mind he would have shot the man dead.

He paused for a moment, panting for breath. He could smell blood and he realized that it was Arturo's blood saturating his shirt. He laid the automatic down for a second and tore off the shirt in disgust. He mopped his friend's blood from his bare chest before he threw the shirt away and picked up the automatic again.

Then he thought to look for Orlando.

Savas had reached the main deck and was searching for a position he could defend. The shadow of a long jib fell over him and he glanced up at one of the tall cranes. The cab of the crane offered an ideal refuge and he slung his submachine gun over his shoulder and scrambled up the steel-runged ladder towards it. Once inside he sat in the driving seat with a commanding view of the working deck and the companionways leading up the main superstructure.

He felt a spasm of emotional anguish as he realized abruptly that Luis was no longer behind him. He looked for the man he loved but the deck below was empty.

He started to climb out of the crane, but then he saw movement along the upper level of the companionways and remained still. He unslung his submachine gun and held it ready.

Regan had reached the third deck level when the stream of nine-millimeter slugs screamed viciously towards him. He was already moving forward and he dived flat. The wooden handrail above his head was splintered to matchwood and the window in the bulkhead behind him showered him with broken glass. The slugs ricocheted whining off steel and one ripped open the shoulder of his flak jacket.

As he dived he had seen the split second of movement in the cab of the crane. He wriggled forward, pushed the barrel of his rifle over the edge of the deck and fired down. The cab windows caved in but he couldn't be sure that he had hit the man.

He squirmed another three yards along the gangway and then risked a quick raise of his head. The submachine gun opened up again and he slammed his cheek back to the deckboards.

His heart was hammering almost as much as the gun.

The man in the cab of the crane was still very much alive.

Nicolson had also dived flat. He could see that Regan was pinned down, and that the man in the crane was also trapped now that he had revealed his position. To attempt any further movement in the open would be suicide and so he looked for a way inside the superstructure. There was a door behind him and he wriggled back to it. Cautiously he raised himself to push the door open and then he ducked inside.

He straightened up in the safety of an interior corridor and pressed the speech button on his radio.

"Steve, keep your head down but keep him occupied. I'll try to work my way around him and then draw his fire."

"Understood." Regan's voice came back strained and tense.

Nicolson ran in search of a stairway, found one and descended rapidly to the main deck level. He was alert to the fact that there was still the second terrorist to be accounted for, but he saw and heard no one. He found a door that brought him out on to the starboard side of the accommodation block on the main deck and eased his way forward to glance round the corner.

There was another exchange of gunfire between Regan and the man in the crane which was on the port side of the deck. Nicolson risked a quick dash into the open and threw himself behind the machinery of a winch. No bullets pursued him. The man in the crane was concentrating on Regan.

Gritting his teeth Nicolson drew himself up on to his hands and knees and made another crouching run. He fell behind a rack of steel piping and banged his stiff leg. He lay softly cursing for a few seconds and then took the third plunge. He was limping badly but he made it to the cover of the raised rotary table in the center of the deck. He looked up at the cab of the crane but the man inside was hidden below the level of the shattered windows.

"Steve," Nicolson whispered into the radio.

"Listening," Regan's voice was a murmur.

"On the count of three. One, two—"

Nicolson didn't finish but sprang into the open. He had both arms stretched up and forward as he fired three fast shots from the Smith & Wesson at the cab of the crane.

Savas saw him through a gap in the steel plates of the cab. Nicolson was a standing target that Savas couldn't miss. He had no fear of the relatively puny automatic, but to bring his submachine gun to bear he had to stand up for a fleeting moment to aim down. As he did so Steve Regan shot the top of his head off with a final burst from the automatic rifle.

Cobral saw Orlando's head disintegrate. Both the friends who had followed him so faithfully across half the world were dead and suddenly there was red anger in his heart. From his position in the radio shack he couldn't see either Regan or Nicolson, but he knew that the man who had fired the fatal shots was somewhere above him.

He moved warily out of his refuge, forgetting the radio operator he had kept alive as a possible hostage. Now vengeance was more important than a last vain gesture to the world revolution.

He began to stalk the man on the companionways above.

Regan had discarded the empty rifle and drawn his Colt .45. He stood up slowly and looked down. The dead man still hung out of the door of the crane. Nicolson had vanished again but Regan thought that he had ducked back behind the rotary table.

Regan remembered that there was still one surviving terrorist.

He moved along the gangway to the head of the next descending companionway. He couldn't see any movement below. There was total silence over the rig.

He decided to play safe and follow Nicolson's example of moving through the interior. He turned his back on the open deck space below and reached for a doorway.

Cobral had crawled out on to a catwalk and crouched behind a life raft. He saw Regan turn away and immediately straightened up. He raised his automatic and aimed at the back of Regan's neck, just above the collar of the protective flak jacket.

Three things happened simultaneously. Cobral fired, Nicolson shouted from the deck below, and at sea level the drifting tugboat *Bulldog* collided heavily with one of the gigantic legs of Colossus Three.

The wrecked helicopter that was poised on the very edge of the landing pad was tipped over the point of balance by the impact. With Vincenzi's body still inside it plunged down nine hundred feet to explode into a mass of flames as it hit the reeling bridge of *Bulldog*.

NINETEEN

"Steve!"

Regan whirled fast at Nicolson's warning. Colossus Three lurched drunkenly to one side, as though heaved by a tidal wave, and Cobral's first shot missed. Cobral swore as the rig settled back on to an even keel, only to shake violently again from the blast of the explosion at sea level. He was aiming for his second shot with his right hand outstretched, his left hand flung up high to maintain his balance as the rig shifted beneath his feet. His eyes were savage, his handsome face contorted with rage, and the striking cobra on his naked chest was a clear target.

Regan squeezed one fast, accurate shot from the Colt .45.

The bang of the Colt almost drowned the crack of Nicolson's Smith & Wesson .38 as the smaller gun spat fire in the same second.

Cobral was slammed backwards against the rail of the catwalk. He spun over the rail and fell twenty feet to the deck below.

Nicolson walked slowly towards him. Regan descended the remaining companionways at a faster pace and they met on either side of the sprawled body. Cobral lay on his back and each eye of the hooded cobra tattoo had been neatly drilled by a bullet hole, one of slightly larger caliber than the other.

Nicolson looked up at Regan.

"Nice shooting, Colonel," he remarked quietly.

Regan dragged up a smile.

"Thanks, Superintendent, but with you around I guess I needn't have bothered."

They moved over to the edge of the deck and stared down at the sea. *Bulldog* had veered away from the rig but she was well alight and sinking fast. Flames and thick clouds of black smoke poured up from her bridge and foredeck, and the wreckage of the Hiller was still a blazing wreath draped across her bows. Further out *Black Knight* was also drifting helplessly and out of control. The other four tugs appeared unharmed and were maintaining their positions with tight towlines.

Above there were now four Sea Kings hovering against the clouded sky.

Nicolson returned his gaze to the agonies of *Bulldog*.

"That ship weighs the best part of a thousand tons," he said desperately. "If she goes under with the towline still attached then the weight could pull us over. We can still lose this rig."

"Then I guess somebody has to slip that towline," Regan said warily. "But first we have to get back aboard our helicopter."

Ten minutes later the Sea King was hovering directly over the burning tugboat. Regan had donned his silver suit and was praying that it was fireproof as well as protection against the deadly nerve gas that could still be lingering on the death ship below. He buckled up the body harness of the helicopter's lowering line and then nodded to Nicolson who was standing by the winch.

Nicolson looked worried and unhappy, but there was no time to waste and there was no other way. Regan climbed out and Nicolson started the winch to lower him down.

As the rope lengthened the build up of heat from below became more intense. Black smoke billowed around

Regan and blotted his dangling silver figure from view. The sweat began to pour out of him and he felt as though he was being roasted alive. He hung suspended and felt a moment of panic as the hot fumes and gases swirled past him. All that he could see was the oily black smoke and he didn't know what was happening.

Then a shift in the wind cleared the air around him for a few seconds and he began to descend again. He realized that Nicolson had stopped lowering while he had been lost from sight. It was too dangerous to simply drop him blind.

He looked down and saw that he was still on target. The whole forward part of the tugboat was a raging furnace of twenty and thirty foot flames, but the stern deck where Nicolson aimed to set him down was relatively clear. He saw the radio mast and radar scanners suddenly buckle and collapse over the gutted bridge. Then he was enveloped in another wave of smoke and heat.

For half a minute he again swung helplessly at the end of the rope. Even with his own air supply in the cylinder on his back he felt as though he must suffocate and choke. Hell itself could be no hotter and no more horrifying than this. He was not merely sweating now, he was drowning in his own grease. His brain was an overloaded computer that threatened to explode under the massive intake of red agony alerts. He wanted to scream.

His eyes were gummed together and he couldn't see, but he felt that he was being lowered again. He forced his tangled eyelashes apart and saw that momentarily the air was clear around him. The stern deck of the tugboat was coming up fast. Nicolson was lowering carefully but there were heavy seas running and *Bulldog* was nosing bows down into the trough of the wave that was lifting her rump.

Regan landed feet first, allowing his knees to buckle but stopping just short of performing a parachute roll. He knew that he could not afford to tear his suit, and as a grim reminder a contorted corpse sprawled on the deckboards by the scuppers. The vomit around the dead man's mouth indicated that he had died from the nerve gas and not from the effects of the fire.

Nicolson had paid out a few feet of slack line to give Regan freedom to work. Regan looked forward and faced a seemingly solid wall of heat and flame and smoke, but the thick towline from Colossus Three lay at his feet and he could see where it ended in a heavy steel eye that was dropped over *Bulldog's* massive, spring-loaded towing hook. With one arm raised to shield his face mask from the flames that licked around him he stumbled towards the hook, knowing that if he could not do the job quickly he would never do it.

Trying to lift the steel eye of the towline was like trying to lift a ton weight. He was attempting the impossible in the heart of an inferno and his struggles became weaker. He was on the point of collapse when he made a last, superhuman effort, and the sea surged in his favour. *Bulldog* dropped in the trough of another wave, riding momentarily backwards, and the towline slackened. The eye came clear of the hook as Regan heaved and then it crashed to the deck at his feet. Like a black snake the towline wriggled rapidly over the stern and vanished beneath the waves.

Regan staggered after it, away from the heat.

"Mark," he croaked into his radio. "Haul me up."

Seconds later he was airborne again, swinging below the helicopter as *Bulldog* disappeared beneath the North Sea in a great hiss of steam.

Black Knight was still a danger, a floating coffin that threatened to foul the rig. Regan rested and then he was lowered again. He picked his way over more horrific corpses littering the deck, but this time it was almost easy without the fire. He could afford to wait for the sea to provide another favourable moment before casting off the second towline.

He faced one final ordeal. He was ducked twice beneath the waves to wash clean any possible traces of the nerve gas that could now be deposited on his suit, and then he was hauled back into the safety of the helicopter. Nicolson helped him out of the suit and then he threw it through the open door. It was US government property but Regan didn't give a damn. He didn't even want to look at it again.

The four surviving tugboats pulled Colossus Three clear of the contaminated area. It was a one-sided tow, but once in safe seas *Boxer* slipped her own towline and steamed in a three quarter circle to pick up the line from the ill-fated *Bulldog*. The skipper of *Dundee Lass*, who was in overall command of the tug fleet, radioed that they now had the giant rig under control on an even tow. They could hold her until replacement tugs arrived to pick up the remaining tow lines.

The flight of Sea Kings headed for home.

It was over and Nicolson wondered why it had ever begun. What could the insane fanatics of Terror Incorporated ever hope to achieve? If world revolution could only succeed by making the world ungovernable, then it would fail. It would have sown the seeds of its own destruction by setting precedents that could only lead by ever bloodier circles into the vortex of world anarchy. Terrorism was a purely negative force. It could destroy but it could not create.

He wondered what Regan thought, but when he turned his head to ask he realized that the answer would have to wait.

The Counter-Terror Section Head for New York was fast asleep.

187